Many of my books are about special friendships. Treasure and India, the two girls in *Secrets*, have one of the closest of these friendships, but on the face of it they are an unlikely pair. They're the same age, they're both bright, bookish girls, they both like drawing and colouring and inventing – but they are worlds apart when it comes to background.

Treasure's had a really scary life. Her mum has a boyfriend who hates Treasure, and vents his temper on her. He might be a good father to his own children, Bethany and Kyle and little Gary, but he threatens poor Treasure, making her life a misery. He goes too far and hits her with his heavy belt, cutting her forehead. Treasure's magnificent, feisty grandma sees this, and sweeps her off to live in her crowded council flat with her own extended family.

India lives nearby, but in a very different huge house. Her father wouldn't dream of hitting her with a belt – but he's too wrapped up in his own affairs to take any notice of her. India's dress designer mother is also absorbed in her own world, frequently impatient with her awkward challenging chubby daughter. India is ultra bright at school, but she makes the other girls groan. They can't understand India, especially her obsession with Anne Frank and her diary. India in her own way is just as much a lonely misfit as Treasure.

I'm the author. I have power over the plot! So of course I made the girls meet and get to know each other properly. They tell their stories in alternate chapters – and when Treasure has to hide away, India is inspired by Anne Frank's diary to offer her a kind of secret annexe.

I'm not really a bit like Treasure *or* India, but we have a few things in common. I was brought up on a big council estate like Treasure, though I never learnt to ride a bike, let alone do wheelies. I was obsessed by Anne Frank like India, reading her very moving diary again and again. I had a photo of Anne by my bedside for years.

Do you think Treasure and India will stay best friends forever? I do hope so.

Jacqueline Wilson

Secrets

Jacqueline Wilson

Illustrated by Nick Sharratt

CORGI YEARLING

SECRETS
A CORGI YEARLING BOOK 978 0 440 86761 6

First published in Great Britain by Doubleday
an imprint of Random House Children's Books

Doubleday edition published 2002
First Corgi Yearling edition published 2003
This Corgi Yearling edition published 2007

5 7 9 10 8 6

Set in Century Schoolbook

Addresses for companies within The Random House Group Limited can be
found at: www.randomhouse.co.uk/offices.htm

THE RANDOM HOUSE GROUP Limited Reg. No. 954009
www.**kids**at**randomhouse**.co.uk

A CIP catalogue record for this book is available from the British Library.

Printed and bound in Great Britain by CPI Bookmarque,
Croydon, CR0 4TD

For Alex – thank you so much for compiling my diary.

One

Treasure

This is the start of my whole new life. I am never going home. I don't ever want to see Mum again. Or Bethany or Kyle or grizzly little Gary. And I especially don't ever, ever, ever want to see Terry.

This notebook used to be the Official Terry Torture Manual. I invented a brand-new torture for him every day. It was a lot of fun. But then sneaky Bethany found the notebook under my pillow and showed it to him. He turned the pages very slowly, taking in all my carefully coloured diagrams of torture machines. I'd spent hours on the Terrible Tooth Tweaker and the Excrutiating Ear Enlarger and the Beastly Big Bum-Basher.

Terry looked at them. He nodded. He drew in his

breath. Then he ripped the pages out and tore them up into tiny pieces. It was obvious he wanted to tear me into tiny pieces too.

Mum tried to turn it into a joke and pretended it was just my warped sense of humour.

'That kid of yours is warped all right,' said Terry. He stood up and unbuckled the heavy leather belt round his jeans. 'She needs teaching a lesson once and for all.'

Mum tried to laugh him out of it, acting like he was just kidding. She said he didn't really mean it. He was just trying to scare me. We were all scared. When he raised the belt Mum yelled at me to run for it. I didn't run fast enough. He got me on the side of my head and broke my glasses and cut me all down my forehead.

Mum cried. Bethany cried because it was all her fault. Kyle cried too though he likes to make out he's so tough. Gary cried, but that's nothing new. I didn't cry. I stood there with blood trickling down into my eyes and I clenched my fists and stared straight at Terry. He looked a bit fuzzy without my specs but he's got these really cold green eyes that you can't miss. I focused on them. Staring him out. He was the one who broke first. He looked away, ducking his head like he was ashamed.

He went straight out down the pub even though Nan and Loretta and her little Britney and Willie and Patsy were coming round for tea. It was all laid out on the living-room table: ham sandwiches and sausage rolls and leftover chocolate log and mince pies and fruit cake, though Kyle and I had nicked most of the icing. Bethany's off sweet stuff at the moment because she thinks she's fat. Well she *is*. I annoy her no end because I eat heaps and stay thin as a pin. Mum says it's my nervous energy.

No wonder I get nervous living with Terry.

But I don't live with him any more, hurray, hurray, hurray! He did me a huge favour hitting me with his belt. Nan took one look at me and went white.

'My God, Treasure, what have they done to you?'

I just shrugged. I'm not a tell-tale like *some* people. Bethany and Kyle and Mum held their breath. Even little Gary stopped grizzling.

My nan's not daft.

'Terry did it, didn't he?' she said.

Her voice was very quiet in the hushed room. She looked round, her eyes flashing.

'Where is he?'

'He's out, Mum. But it wasn't really Terry's fault. It was an accident.'

'Accident my bottom,' said Nan.

Well, she said something ruder and more alliterative. We have learnt about alliteration at school. I am Top Girl. Which isn't hard because heaps of our kids have got problems. Our school has got a bad name. But I won't have to go to it any more. I shall go to a school near my nan's. I am living with her now.

I can't believe it! Oh, I love my nan *sooooo* much. She got it all sorted. She made me stand under the light in the living room and gently pushed back my sticky fringe and peeled off the plasters Mum had stuck on. Nan swore again when she saw the size of the cut.

'Go and get your coat, Treasure,' she said quietly.

'What are you on about, Mum?' said my mum.

'We're off,' said Nan. She nodded at the rest of the family. 'Come on. We'll have tea back at our place, once we've taken Treasure up the hospital.'

'Hospital?' Mum whispered.

'She needs stitches, Tammy. How did he *do* it? Did he knife her?'

'No, no, it was an accident, his belt—'

'His belt,' said Nan. She hugged me tight. 'Right. Bethany, you get yourself upstairs with a big carrier bag and get Treasure's clothes packed. She's staying with me from now on.'

We all stared at Nan.

'Jump to it, Bethany!' Nan commanded.

'Yes, Nan,' said Bethany, jumping. She's not *her* nan but she does as Nan tells her. We all do.

'You can't, Mum,' said my mum, starting to cry.

I thought she meant I couldn't stay with Nan. I nearly cried then, because I didn't want Mum to feel I was walking out on her. She needed me. She's useless at keeping Bethany and Kyle under control and she doesn't always get up for Gary in the night. And then there's Terry. He hits her too.

I decided maybe I should stay.

But it turned out she didn't mean that at all.

'You can't take Treasure up the hospital, Mum. They'll want to know how it happened,' my mum sobbed. 'And then they'll get on to the Social – maybe even the police. They'll come down on Terry like a ton of bricks.'

Nan held me even tighter. She could feel me quivering.

'So it's Terry we've got to think of, is it? Our Treasure can get scarred for life but never mind her, let's all worry about Terry?'

Kyle was looking puzzled because he doesn't get sarcasm. Gary was wailing now, his nose running down into his mouth. Mum looked awful too, her mascara smudged and her face so white it made the pink rouge along her cheekbones look like clown make-up.

'It's just a nasty nick,' Mum pleaded. 'Take Treasure for a little holiday, it's maybe all for the best – but don't cause trouble, Mum, I beg you.'

'Call yourself a mother!' said Nan. She bent down, scooped Gary out of his baby chair, checked his nappy and grimaced. 'Here, try and take care of this one at least.' She thrust Gary at Mum and yelled up the stairs to Bethany.

Bethany came running with a carrier bag spilling clothes. Nan snatched it from her and gave my shoulder a squeeze.

'Right, pet, we'll be off.'

Mum was so busy crying she didn't say goodbye to me. Kyle just gawped. But Bethany suddenly put her arms round me and gave me a big hug, even though we've hated each other ever since we've been stepsisters.

'I'm sorry, Treasure,' she said.

She must have been truly sorry because when I unpacked the carrier bag back at Nan's I found she'd put in her own black designer T-shirt, the one with the little grey squirrel on the front. She'd got it as one of her Christmas presents from Terry and she'd gone berserk on Boxing Day when she'd found me secretly trying it on. It fitted perfectly even though I'm nearly two years older, because she's big and I'm a little titch. She had told me to whip it off quick or she'd tell her dad – but now she'd given it to me.

I'm wearing it now with my black jeans and my crocodile boots. I look seriously cool. OK, the boots are last year's and so they scrunch up my toes a bit but I don't care.

'We women have to suffer to look stylish,' says Nan when she kicks her high heels off and rubs her own sore feet.

My nan is young for a grandma and very, very glamorous. She wouldn't be seen dead in the usual granny gear. My nan wears tight, lacy vesty things and short skirts that show off her legs. She looks especially glam when she teaches her line-dancing class. She has all these little matching outfits. I like the white one best: white waistcoat with rhinestones, short white skirt and white leather cowboy boots with spurs.

'Can I go to your line-dancing class sometime, Nan?' I asked her.

'Of course you can, darling. I reckon you'll pick it up in no time. Patsy goes, don't you, pet?'

Patsy grinned at me. 'Yes, it'll be great, Treasure.'

Patsy is being so *kind* to me. She's so, so different from Bethany. Patsy doesn't even seem to mind that she has to share her bedroom with me. It's not much bigger than a cupboard so it isn't easy. She's only got a single bed so Nan fixed me up with cushions and a spare duvet on the floor. It seemed all right to start with but in the middle of the night the cushions kept sliding sideways.

Patsy heard me rootling around, trying to re-organize my bedding. 'Here, Treasure, come in my bed,' she whispered.

'There isn't room. It's OK, I'm fine,' I whispered back.

'No, you're not. Come on, it'll be fun.' She paused and then giggled. 'Do as your auntie says, Treasure!'

I giggled too. Patsy is only seven but she is my actual auntie. She's Nan's youngest child. My mum is the oldest. Though she acts like she's never grown up, Nan always says.

Patsy is Nan's favourite. She calls her 'my little surprise'. She's Pete's child and Nan is nuts about him. I can't remember him properly but I think he's big and bear-like. Patsy is little and fluffy, like a baby bunny. She's got lovely, long fair hair. She wears it in a pony-tail or a topknot with a cute little set of butterfly slides at either side. The only funny thing about Patsy is that she walks with her feet pointing out like a penguin, but that's because she does a lot of ballet. She does tap too and acrobatics. Nan's thinking of sending her to a special stage school soon as she has the talent and the looks to make it really big.

You'd think Patsy would be a horrid little show-off but she's not a bit. I've always liked her lots though we haven't met up much as I've lived all over the place with my mum and then, when Mum settled down with Terry, she and Nan kept falling out. But I like all Nan's family and I love Patsy second-best to Nan.

I squeezed into her bed and we cuddled up like spoons. Patsy felt so little and springy compared with Bethany. (We weren't usually on cuddling terms at all but if Terry and my mum were having a fight in the middle of the night it got so scary that Bethany and I would huddle together, the duvet over our heads to block out the noise.)

Patsy's hair tickled my face but I didn't mind. I reached out and stroked it gently. I'm trying to grow my own hair but it goes all wispy. If I tilt my head back and hunch up I can kid myself I've got shoulder-length hair, but it's not really. Patsy is so lucky having lovely long hair. Patsy is so lucky, full stop.

Still, I've got lucky now. This is my new life and I'm happy, happy, happy. I look a bit weird still because I had to have ten stitches and they're still sticking out of my forehead. Nan hasn't dared wash my hair yet so my fringe is all stuck together. I shall have a big scar but I don't care. It will make me look TOUGH.

I didn't tell on Terry up at the hospital. I couldn't do it to Mum. I said me and my brother and sister were

14

messing around playing a stupid cowboy game and I got lassoed.

Nan backed me up.

'Though why we should protect that pig I don't know,' she muttered, lighting up a ciggie. 'Still, I'm not having anyone call *me* a grass.'

She got told that the hospital has a strictly no-smoking policy so she stamped on it. She looked like she wanted to grind Terry under her high heel too.

'Your mum's the one needs her head looking at,' said Nan, as we trailed out the hospital, my forehead all puckered up with black thread. 'Why doesn't she *leave* him?'

I shrugged. It baffles me too. 'Still, *I've* left him now, haven't I, Nan?' I said.

'You bet, Treasure. You were such a good brave girl up the hospital. I'm proud of you.'

'And I can really, truly stay with you, Nan? I'll do lots of housework and keep an eye on Patsy and I could help Loretta with little Britney, I'm good with babies—'

'Bless you, pet,' said Nan. 'You don't have to earn your keep. You're *family*.'

'And I can stay in your family for good, Nan? Promise?'

'Yes, I promise, Treasure,' said Nan.

That's the best bit. You can rely on my nan. She never, ever breaks her promises.

Two

India

Dear Kitty

I don't know what to put! And it sounds a bit silly, 'Dear Kitty' – as if I'm writing a letter to our cat, Tabitha. I started this new diary that way because that's how Anne Frank wrote *her* diary. She was this wonderful Jewish girl who had to hide in a secret annexe with her family during the last world war, and while she was there she wrote a diary. She was a brilliant writer. She described everything so vividly. You really feel you're hiding in the annexe with her, sharing your bedroom with a grumpy old dentist, eating rotten vegetables, running out of clothes to wear and having to creep about all the time, not even able to pull the lavatory chain when anyone's downstairs.

Well, I don't flush the toilet sometimes when I get up in the night, but that's because our water system's really noisy and it wakes everyone up. If Dad wakes up he can't get back to sleep because he's under a lot of pressure at work. That sounds so funny, as if Dad sits at his desk with a huge weight on his head. Actually he often rubs the back of his neck now as if it's hurting him.

It hurts me too. I really love my dad. He's a managing director of this big engineering firm, Major Products. I don't really know what major things they produce. I don't even know exactly what my dad does. He manages. He directs. He's always been a whizz at his job but now he acts like he's worried all the time. I tried massaging his neck for him yesterday but he pushed my hands away and said, 'Stop *dabbing* at me, India.'

I went away and cried. Mum happened to be home and came in to my bedroom to look for my coat and skirt to send to the cleaners.

'Maybe I'd better send you to the cleaners too, India,' she said, looking at my blotchy face and inky fingers. I'd written a poem to express my feelings. It started *Oh woe, I love my Dad so*. It wasn't one of my *better* poems.

Mum asked why I was crying, even sitting on the bed beside me and acting all *mumsie* for once. She seemed disappointed when I told her it was because Dad didn't seem to want me around him any more.

'For God's sake, India, don't be such a baby,' she

said, laughing at me. 'He just snapped at you, that's all. That's nothing. You should hear the things he says to me sometimes.'

She sniffed resentfully. Then she smiled again. Mum has this really irritating, dazzling smile showing off all her cosmetic dentistry – but her eyes don't light up. It's as if her face is a mask and her eyes are the only real bit.

'Still, I suppose we'd better try to be understanding. Dad's having a hard time at work.' Mum sighed. 'Aren't we all?' The smile was still there but it was as if she was silently adding, 'But *some* of us cope without making all this fuss.'

Anne Frank loved her dad but frequently couldn't bear her mother. I feel Anne and I are soul sisters. I love to write too. I write my diary, I write stories and poems, I even wrote the nativity play at school. I tried so hard, rewriting it three whole times, trying to be *original*, so it was mostly from the animals' point of view, with the ox and the ass and the littlest lamb as the major characters.

Mrs Gibbs said in class that it was 'a lovely idea, don't you think so, girls?' Everyone smiled and said it was super. But out in the playground they all groaned and made faces and said it was the most stupid idea ever and who wanted to act as a cow, for God's sake? Did I think they were all *babies*?

I should have said they were all acting like babies right that minute. I didn't. I just blushed and stammered and said I was sorry, yes it was a mad idea, in fact it absolutely sucked. So then they despised me for being wet as well as babyish and a teacher's pet. Sometimes I think I despise myself.

I have bright ginger hair. Most people think this means I have a fearful temper. I do get angry inside but I can't stick up for myself. I only get furious when I think things aren't fair for other people.

Maria waited until the others had all run off and then she put her arm round me and said she thought my play sounded very imaginative. It was maybe more suited to *little* children. She thought it would work a treat with them.

Maria was probably just being kind though. She's kind to everyone.

I wish Maria was my friend but she's Alice's best friend. *Everyone* in my class has got a best friend – or else they go round in little gangs like Lucy and Imogen and Sarah and Claudia. It's so awful not having a gang, not having a best friend.

I *used* to. I used to have Miranda. We knew each other right from when we were babies because we shared the same nanny while our mums ran this designer scarf company. Miranda and I were almost like sisters. We went to the same kindergarten and then the same school. We always had each other.

Miranda could be just a bit boring sometimes because she never had any ideas of her own – but I always had *heaps* of ideas so I suppose it didn't matter too much. Miranda wasn't much use at playing pretend games but at least she didn't laugh at me.

When we were little we had two favourites: we played Monkeys, swinging about and being silly and scratching ourselves, or we played the Flying Game, pretending the sleeves of our coats were wings and swooping around all over the place. I know, it sounds so daft now, but we were *very* little.

As we got a bit older the two games merged. Flying Monkeys was the best game of all. We pretended we could whizz through open windows and throw peanuts at people. We could ride the weathercock on the church steeple, prance on the roof of the tallest multi-storey and nest in the tops of the poplars on the playing fields. We Flying Monkeys fiercely defended our territory against our enemies, Flying Elephants flapping their vast ears.

Mum saw us battling it out one day. She didn't understand this was Flying Animal Warfare. She clapped her hands and said, 'That looks great fun, girls' but when she got me on my own she hissed, 'I wish you wouldn't *shriek* so, India. And do you really have to galumph around like that?'

I said sulkily that I was being an elephant so I was *supposed* to galumph.

Mum said, 'Oh, I *see*, my little Indian elephant.'

If Dad had said it he would have been making a funny joke. But Mum was getting at me. She can't stand it because I'm fat. She's never actually *said* it. The nearest we come to it is 'large', as in, 'My daughter's a little on the *large* side.' She whispers the word as if it's obscene. She thinks it is.

My mum is so skinny her arms and legs look like you could snap them in half. When she wears a low-cut top you can see all her bones. OK, she's got a fabulous flat tummy but she's flat *everywhere*. She isn't naturally thin. She is on a permanent diet. She doesn't *say* she's dieting. She says she eats perfectly normally. It isn't normal to eat fruit and salad and raw vegetables all the time. I know she loves cakes and chocolate like everyone else but she never weakens. Dad once bought us a special big cake from a Viennese patisserie. Mum smiled and said, 'How *gorgeous*!' And then had ONE bite of her slice. It was a little bite too. She's the same with chocolates. I've seen her *lick* one white Belgian cream chocolate and then throw it in the bin. She is amazing. I could never do that. I am the exact opposite. I could eat an entire great gateau and a giant box of chocolates all by myself, easy-peasy.

Mum and I have this constant battle. I am supposed to be on a diet but I don't stick to it. I eat my slither of chicken and my cherry tomatoes and my carrot sticks and my apple and my orange – and then I sneak upstairs and munch two Mars Bars and crunch a whole pack of Pringles.

Mum went bananas when she found all the empty wrappings under my bed. She shouted all sorts of stuff and I cried and that made her worse because she hates me being a cry-baby. She was furious with Wanda for letting me buy them. Wanda cried too.

Wanda is even more of a cry-baby than I am. Wanda is our latest au pair. We've had lots since I stopped needing a nanny. They never stay long. Mum never likes them. Dad likes the pretty ones so Mum gets rid of them sharpish. Mum and Dad had a big fight over Brigitte. And Selke. And Mai. So Mum decided to try an Australian girl.

'Someone sunny-natured and strong,' said Mum.

'And bronzed and bouncy and blonde!' Dad whispered to me, and we both giggled.

But the laugh was on us, because Wanda isn't at all the way we wanted her to be. She's certainly not sunny. She looks vague and misty most of the time, so the kindest way of describing her would be cloudy. When she cries she's downright dismal. She isn't strong. She can't manage more than one bag of shopping and she's always yawning and flopping down on the sofa and falling asleep. She's not bronzed and bouncy and blonde. She's papery-white and droopy, with long, dark, witchy hair. She washes it once a day, sometimes even twice, and walks around with it dripping wet.

Wanda takes me to school and fetches me in the afternoon and fixes me a few snacks. We've done a little deal. We chuck the cottage cheese and celery and carrots straight in the bin and buy secret supplies of sweets and stuff. It's not fair. Wanda eats as much chocolate and crisps as I do and yet she's ever so thin, even thinner than Mum.

Mum hoped she might use Wanda as a cheap personal assistant, taking phone calls and collecting material samples and contacting models, but Wanda wisely made such a mess of things Mum's banned her from having anything to do with the business.

My mum is Moya Upton, the children's clothes designer. She swapped from scarves five years ago, when she couldn't find any clothes she liked for me. So now *she* makes ultra-cool designer clothes for kids. There are three Moya Upton shops in London – in Notting Hill, South Kensington and Hampstead – one in Leeds, one in Glasgow, and there's a special Moya Upton section in Harrods' Junior Collection department. There was a five-page feature in *Vogue* last year, and heaps of stuff in the papers. All the girls in my school are mad about Moya Upton clothes.

The only girl in the entire country who *hates* Moya Upton clothes is me. They are little and I am big. They are tight and I need loose. They are bright and I like dark. They are sparkly and I like stark. My mum always says she started designing clothes to suit her daughter. I don't know which daughter that is. It certainly isn't me.

Three

Treasure

The first few days I got scared every time there was a knock on the door in case it was Mum ready to take me back. I got scared a lot, because Nan is seriously popular and everyone keeps popping round to have a natter with Rita. That's Nan's name.

Everyone treats my nan like they want to be her best friend. She got nearly two hundred Christmas cards; Patsy and I counted them. Nan sticks them up all over the walls with Blu-tack so they look like festive wall-paper. Nan does Christmas so beautifully. There's a big tree with glass balls and sugar cane candy and tinsel and fairy lights and a fairy doll tied to the top. She's got wings and a wand with a little silver star. Loretta's baby Britney absolutely adores the

Christmas tree. I pick her up and walk her round and round and she waves her little hands. She likes the fairy doll best of all, reaching up to try and take hold of her, cheeping like a little bird.

'Yes, darling, the fairy!' I go, and I whirl her around as if *she's* got fairy wings and is flying through the air. 'Shall we make a fairy wish, Britney?' I say, and I whisper in the tiny whorls of her ear. 'You want your cousin Treasure to stay here for ever and ever, don't you?' I nod my head vigorously and she nods too. I make a bulgy bug-eyed face as if I'm wishing like crazy. Britney laughs and I go, 'Ping!' as if the fairy doll has really waved her pipecleaner wand.

'You shouldn't keep picking her up like that. She'll only whine when you strap her back in her baby chair,' said Loretta.

She doesn't always like me playing with Britney. Loretta sometimes gets fussed when *Nan* picks her up. Loretta likes to do everything herself, so that Britney likes her best. It's a bit silly though, because she's always tired out, with dark circles round her eyes. She always lies down when Britney has a nap and she gets dead ratty if Patsy and I are playing some game and wake her up.

'Loretta's feeling a bit down at the moment,' Nan whispered to me. 'Don't worry, it'll pass.'

'Is it because Britney's dad doesn't want to know?' I whispered back.

Nan shrugged. 'Maybe.'

I nodded and tutted like I understood, all girls

together – but I think Loretta's *mad*. Boyfriends are Big Trouble. You don't need them. But babies are lovely. I'm going to have lots when I'm old enough. I told Nan and she laughed.

'Steady on. You're the bright one of the family, Treasure. Don't you want to go on to university, be a career girl, eh?'

'I could be a mum *and* a career girl,' I said.

'That's it, Treasure, think big,' said Nan.

'Think *Bighead*,' said Willie, and he bounced his football right at me.

'Watch her new glasses!' Nan shrieked, and she caught the ball and aimed it at Willie's head. Hard.

Nan took me down the optician's, a posh one where they make your glasses there and then, and now I've got brand new specs, little oval metal ones, *designer*!

I don't look quite so awful in them. I truly don't. If only my hair would grow I might start to look pretty. Maybe I'm going to take after Nan as I get older.

'Old Speccy Four-Eyes,' Willie chants, but I don't give a stuff about him.

'Old Pimple Bum-Fuzz,' I yell back, which really riles him.

'You buzz off back home where you belong,' he said.

'I belong here now,' I said.

I don't care that Willie doesn't want me. Or Loretta. Little Britney likes me. Patsy likes me lots. And my nan loves me and says I'm her little Treasure. I love

Nan so very, very much. But like I said, everyone loves her.

We had this BIG New Year's Eve party last night and I couldn't believe the number of people who were squashed up in the flat at twelve o'clock. It was just like the tube in the rush hour, only there everyone has glum faces and keeps quiet, whereas here everyone was happy, happy, happy, bouncing about and laughing and dancing and drinking.

I got to stay up too – and Patsy. Even little Britney made it past midnight. Loretta didn't mind me holding her because she was dancing all the time. She had a new tiny purple skirt and a tight red top and she suddenly looked great. She's a fantastic dancer too, obviously taking after Nan. Oh, you should have seen my nan dancing! She looked wonderful in a slinky black dress, low-cut and short so she showed off her legs. Everyone went on at her to demonstrate a spot of line dancing so she did this lovely routine to Shania's *From This Moment* and half her dance class joined in, everyone else squashing into corners and sitting six-deep on the sofa to make room on the floor.

Then Nan and Loretta and Patsy did *Red Hot Salsa*, hands on hips and wiggling their bottoms. Patsy was especially good, giving a little wink every time she wiggled that made everyone roar with laughter. Nan danced on her own to Tom Jones' *Sex Bomb* and everyone clapped like crazy and said Nan was a Sex Bomb all right. They wanted her to go on and on but Nan insisted everyone dance to ordinary disco music.

She did too, but sort of *fancy*, so you still couldn't take your eyes off her. She saw me watching and beckoned me up on the floor with her and danced me round and round with her, quicker and quicker until I started wheezing and my glasses steamed up.

I had to have a little puff of my Ventolin then and Nan said I should maybe take it easy, but then it was midnight and we all jumped up and down and screamed, and there was so much *kissing*! *Willie* kissed me, but he kissed every girl in the room. He'd been drinking a lot of lager and then he had pink champagne at midnight. *I* had pink champagne too, half a glass full. I felt as if all the little pink bubbles were fizzing in my head.

Then the phone started ringing and I got scared in case it was my mum but it was just my Auntie Dolly, Nan's second eldest, ringing up from Wales. Then Uncle Waylon rang from Sydney in Australia, and then some cousins rang, and some of Nan's friends. The phone kept ringing and ringing. I got so used to it I stopped jumping every time and thinking it was Mum. In fact a very strange thing happened. I started kind of hoping it *might* be Mum.

Don't get me wrong. I love it here at Nan's and I don't ever, ever, ever want to go back home. It's just I started wondering why my mum doesn't want me back. Doesn't she even want to know how I'm getting on? Isn't she worried about my cut? Why didn't she want to wish me a happy new year? There were people ringing from the other side of the world.

Couldn't my mum be bothered to ring from the other side of London?

Patsy saw I looked a bit down and asked if I had a headache from drinking the pink champagne. She was convinced we'd get dreadful hangovers even though we only had a few sips each. Nan was surrounded by all these stupid men wanting to kiss her but she spotted me in the corner and came and gave me a cuddle.

I didn't tell her what was wrong. I didn't have to.

'Do you want to ring your mum, sweetheart?' she whispered.

I nodded. Then I shook my head. Then I shrugged.

Nan seemed to understand that too.

'You have a little think about it, darling. You could always ring tomorrow, eh, just in case she's gone to bed tonight. And you don't want to risk talking to that *animal*, do you?'

'*Definitely* not.'

I cheered up a little deciding precisely which species of animal Terry might belong to. I fancied the idea of a hippopotamus because they're big and fat and ugly and they yawn a lot showing all their teeth – and according to this nature film I saw on the telly they spray their dung about in a totally disgusting manner.

There were all sorts of bangs and whizzes outside from fireworks so Nan said we could watch them from her bedroom in the front of the house. I wanted to show little Britney but she'd curled up fast asleep in a corner, all cuddled up with Nan's turquoise furry python doorstop. She looked *so* cute.

Willie was chatting with some of the big boys in the kitchen (and drinking more lager) so it was just Patsy and me. It's a big treat going into Nan's bedroom because it's all red velvet and pink satin with lovely pictures of cherubs on the walls and a big gilt dressing-table with all Nan's make-up and scent bottles and a proper matching silver hairbrush and mirror set decorated with little cherub heads. I asked Nan if they were a really valuable antique and she cracked up laughing and said, '*I'm* the only really valuable antique in this flat, Treasure.'

But Nan doesn't look a bit old. She looks very young. She and my mum could be sisters. In fact when Nan's all dressed up and Mum's all white and worried and needing to wash her hair then it looks like *Nan* is my mum's daughter. And then Nan could be my mum and *I'd* be Patsy so I'd be pretty and sweet and talented. I wouldn't wear glasses and have a pinched face and limp hair. I wouldn't think weird things and get on everyone's nerves.

Patsy tied up the pink ruffles on Nan's curtains and we stared out at the fireworks shooting up into the sky.

'Wow!' said Patsy. 'Wow! Wow! Wow!'

She started to get on my nerves. She sounded like a little dog. The fireworks were so beautiful they made my chest ache. I shook every time another rocket exploded. I stared until my eyes went blurry.

'Are you crying, Treasure?' Patsy asked, peering at me in the dim light.

'Of course not.'

'You are. Does your forehead hurt?'

'It's OK.'

'It must be so weird being all stitched up like that. How come they used that ugly black thread?' She touched one of the stitches very gently, shuddering a little.

'They don't fuss about the colour. They just want to stop all the blood leaking out.'

'Yuck. He's so horrible, Uncle Terry. How could he do that to you?'

'He's done worse. He's not *Uncle* Terry, though. He's nothing.'

'I'm *Auntie* Patsy.'

'Yeah, right, we've done all that bit.'

Another rocket exploded, another and another, the whole sky raining pink and green and gold, and Patsy did her dainty little doggy, 'Wow! Wow! Wow!'

'It's better than Bonfire Night, isn't it?' she said, leaning against me. 'I wonder who's letting them off? I suppose it's all those posh nobs up in Parkfield.' She said the name slowly and softly, but with great emphasis, as if it was the most special place in all the world. Forget London, New York, San Francisco, Sydney – Parkfield's the place.

I humoured her. 'What's Parkfield?'

'It's this estate. Not council, it's private, huge, and you should see the *houses*. They're enormous with masses of bedrooms and bathrooms. Mum says some have got swimming pools in the basements; imagine! That's where I'm going to live when I'm grown up, Treasure.'

'Oh yeah?'

'Well, I *could*, you know, if I make it in show biz. All these actors and singers and dancers live up Parkfield. That actress from *EastEnders*, *she* lives there now. There was a whole feature about her in *OK* magazine, Mum showed me. *I'm* going to get in *OK* one day. Maybe for my wedding, eh, and I'll wear white, of course, and me and my husband will sit on thrones and tell you what, Treasure, you could be my bridesmaid.'

I leant my forehead against the cold glass, letting her prattle on while the fireworks flashed.

'What about you, Treasure? What sort of wedding are you going to have? Shall I be *your* bridesmaid?'

'I'm not ever, ever, ever going to get married,' I said.

'Why not?' Patsy misunderstood. 'You'll maybe grow up to be prettier. And you could wear contact lenses.'

'I don't *want* to get married. I don't want a stupid scary mean old husband, thanks.'

Patsy thought about it. 'You'll need a career then,' she said. 'What do you want to be, eh?'

'I don't know.'

'*I've* known I want to be a dancer – or an actress – or a singer – since I was *three*,' Patsy said proudly. She waited. 'Hey, I didn't mean it to sound like I was showing off. I know, Treasure, you can be some big posh business lady who earns a fortune. Mum says you're dead brainy, *much* brainier than me. OK? Then *you* could live in Parkfield too. We could have adjoining houses, you and me.'

Yeah, sure. Dream on, Patsy. You might get to live in this posh Parkfield. I haven't got a chance.

Four

India

Dear Kitty

I don't think I like this year one bit. It's no better than the last year. It's WORSE.

I've broken my resolutions already. In fact I broke the first resolution within ten minutes. I was supposed to go on a diet: *Sensible Eating for Sparky Kids*. It's a book. One of my mum's friends wrote it. She's got this son, Ben, and he's fat too. He gets called Big Ben at school.

Mum thought Ben and I might bond because of this and so she invited them to our New Year's party.

'I want you to be a good little hostess and keep a special eye on Ben,' said Mum.

'Oh, Mum, that's so mean. I don't want to get

stuck with any boy. Especially Ben,' I wailed.

I make out I can't stand boys. If I'm honest I suppose this is because they mostly can't stand *me*. Anne Frank and I are poles apart on this one. She was ever so popular and had heaps of boyfriends. I haven't ever had any.

Ben and I have never really hit it off. He used to push me off my toddler trike when we were little and he once tore the head off my Barbie doll, deliberately. I hadn't seen him for a year or two and wondered if he might have improved. Mum said he was fatter than ever and utterly refusing to go on his mum's diet. I decided we might have something in common after all.

Ben certainly was wonderfully enormous, stuffed into a big denim shirt and combat trousers. They were supposed to look baggy but they were very close fitting on Ben. I did my best to be a Good Hostess. I offered him a drink and several snacks and tried to make small talk. The talk got smaller and smaller, threatening to dwindle into silence. I asked him what subjects he liked most at school. And then wanted to know his favourite television programmes. And what type of mobile phone he had.

'Look, is this some dumb questionnaire?' he said.

'No, I was just trying to make conversation,' I said, mortified.

'You don't have to hang around me, India.'

'I don't mind,' I mumbled.

'Yes, but I do,' he said – and he went off and started chatting to Phoebe.

Phoebe is my mum's favourite model. She is a year younger than me but she acts like she's ages older. She has a mass of wonderful soft black curls, big, big, big eyes with long lashes, and she's *tiny*. She is so beautiful it makes me ache to look at her. Even Mum softens when she speaks to Phoebe. Her voice goes all gooey and sickeningly sweet.

Thank goodness Dad doesn't go a bundle on Phoebe.

'She looks like Bambi with a wig on,' he whispered to me the first time we met her. I got the giggles so badly I snorted and stuff came out my nose.

I looked for Dad at the party but he didn't seem to want me hanging round him either. He had a bottle of whisky in one hand and Wanda's au pair friend, Suzi, in the other. Wanda herself had e-mailed her family in Australia and then retreated to her room, crying. I suppose she was homesick. I wasn't allowed to go to *my* room. I had to stand there with a stupid smile on my face, passing round the party snacks.

I told people again and again and again that my name is India and yes I *am* Moya's daughter and I *am* getting a big girl now. It got so bad I wanted to scream and throw the canapés at them. I snacked a lot myself. Caviar looks like baby blackberries so I expected it to taste sweet. I took a big bite and wrinkled my face in disgust. Mum said it's an acquired taste. I don't think I'll ever acquire a taste for rotting fish. Mum got a black bead of caviar stuck between her front teeth. I didn't tell her.

At twelve o'clock everyone went mad and started kissing. Ben kissed Phoebe. He didn't kiss me. Dad kissed me and some of Mum's friends kissed me and one silly man picked me up and whirled me round and round and then got very red in the face and had to sit down. Mum frowned at me as if it was *my* fault. Mum did her fair share of kissing too. The black bit of caviar had gone. Some sad person had it stuck to their tongue, yuck yuck.

I looked closely at all the smiling men, trying to spot which one.

'Don't *peer* like that, India,' Mum hissed. Then there was a loud swoop and bang and Mum clapped her hands like a little girl.

'Firework time!' she cried. 'Goodie goodie!'

She ushered everyone into the garden to watch. She'd hired a firework man to do a special display. We had to stand behind the little picket fence for safety, so we were uncomfortably huddled together. I saw Dad making the most of this with Suzi. I wished she hadn't come to the party. I wanted Dad to myself. Mum was bobbing about in the distance. I edged further and further away from her. I knew it would annoy her if she saw me standing all by myself.

I peered up at all the rockets and each time one burst into stars I made a wish.

I wish I had a real best friend!

I wished it ten times over and then I crept back inside the house, into the kitchen. The left-over party canapés were congealing on their silver trays.

'Blow *Sensible Eating*. I'm *not* a *Sparky Kid*,' I muttered. I ate every single honey-glazed sausage and asparagus tip and quail's egg and goat's cheese tartlet and Thai chicken stick and *even* the caviar canapés, and *then* I went to the fridge and got a big carton of Loseley vanilla-and-ginger ice-cream and ate the lot. Then I went up to bed.

I wasn't sick. I *felt* sick – and I got up in the night to go to the bathroom just in case. The party seemed to have finished because it was quiet downstairs. It was very noisy in Mum and Dad's bedroom. They seemed to be having a serious quarrel about Suzi.

I felt so lonely I wondered about going into Wanda's room. If she was still crying we could maybe comfort each other. But when I peeped round her door I saw she was fast asleep, her hair inky-black against her pillow, her long feet sticking straight out the end of her duvet. I decided it would be mean to wake her so I trailed back to my own bed and put the light on and started reading Anne Frank's diary all over again to take my mind off my queasy stomach.

The first part made me feel sadder than ever because Anne had so many friends when she was at school, before she had to go into hiding.

Maybe we're not soulmates after all.

I absolutely *have* to get a proper best friend at school this year. I shall try harder with Maria. Maybe she'll let me be her second-best friend. She might even get fed up with Alice and want to go around with *me*.

* * *

I can't believe I wrote that. I HATE Maria now.

I tried very, very hard the first day back at school. I sit over the other side of the classroom from Maria and Alice but I hovered by their desks before lessons and after lessons. I went along to the girls' cloakrooms when they did and stood in the lunch queue with them, listening all the time. Whenever Maria said anything – for example:

a) I got a new mobile phone for Christmas.
b) I'm seriously thinking of becoming a vegetarian.
c) Wasn't *Buffy* good last night?

I'd say:

a) I'm going to ask for a mobile for my birthday. I'll buy it all these little covers so it's like it's my doll and I can dress it up. Wouldn't it be weird if your mobile developed its own personality and only let you chat to the people it really liked? It would tell everyone else to get lost in this funny little electronic voice.

b) I'm thinking about being a vegetarian too. I especially can't stand the idea of eating lamb, can you, as they look so sweet – but it's a bit unfair to think it's OK to eat really hideous animals like eels – not that anyone in their right mind would want to. And they eat snakes somewhere, don't they? Imagine!

c) *Buffy* is my all-time favourite programme. Do you think there really are vampires?

Wouldn't it be great to be the chosen one?
Mind you, it would be pretty exciting to be a
vampire too.

I thought my replies were a lot more interesting
than Alice's, which were:

   a) You are lucky.
   b) Me too.
   c) Yeah.

But somehow Maria didn't seem to think so. She
started off the day nodding and smiling but by the
time we were packing our bags ready to go home
she was shaking her head and frowning all over her
face. She didn't *say* anything and when I said goodbye
she said goodbye back. Alice said goodbye too – but
then she added 'and good riddance!' the moment I'd
turned my back. Maria went, 'Alice!' like that – but she
burst out laughing. They both did.

I walked across the playground with my head held
high, pretending not to have heard them. I shan't go
near them tomorrow. I've never been that keen on
Alice but I thought Maria might be different.

I'm the one who's different.

I wish everyone didn't think I'm weird.

Wanda was waiting for me, leaning against the rail-
ings and inspecting her nose in her pocket mirror. She
hasn't put on an ounce of weight with all the chocolates she eats but she hasn't half got spotty.

Maria and Alice brushed past us, giggling like
anything.

'Why are you blushing, India?' said Wanda.

'I'm not!' I said, stupidly.

Wanda held her mirror up. I saw a flash of Boiled Lobster Girl.

'I've been running. I'm hot,' I said, though it was so cold I was huddled right up inside my duffel coat. It's part of the school uniform. Unlike every other girl in our school I actually *like* the old-fashioned uniform. Especially the duffel coat. Dad always calls me his little Paddington Bear when I wear it.

Well, he *did*. He doesn't call me anything now. He doesn't seem to notice me most of the time. When he *does* I just seem to get on his nerves.

He came across me sitting on the stairs reading Anne Frank's diary. He tripped over me, actually. He asked if he'd hurt me and I shook my head, although he did a bit. I think I've got a bruise on my bottom where his foot accidentally kicked me. I can't be sure though because I never have a proper look at my bottom. It's too depressing.

'So why are you looking so miserable then?' Dad said, peering down at me.

I sighed deeply, wondering where to start. I hoped Dad would sit down beside me but he stayed looming over my head. I began to tell him about Maria and Alice but after a sentence or two he started fidgeting.

'I'm sure you'll all make friends again soon. Why don't you ask them both round to play?' said Dad, starting to go downstairs.

'We don't *play*,' I said, offended. 'And I haven't ever *been* friends with Maria, that's the point. I haven't *got* a proper friend at my horrible old school.'

'Well, maybe you'll be going to a new school soon,' said Dad.

I peered at him, trying to see his face in the gloom of the stairwell. He didn't sound as if he was joking.

What did he mean, a new school? I suddenly got tremendously worried. Maybe Dad and Mum were planning to send me to boarding school? Perhaps they'd got sick of me being in the way?

Miranda goes to boarding school now. She *wanted* to go. She loves the *Harry Potter* books and thought the whole boarding school idea would be wonderful – but she positively hated it at first. She wept buckets – tanks – a whole *swimming pool*. The letter she wrote to me was all tear-stained and smudgy. OK, she says it's not so bad now. In fact last time she wrote to me she said it was great. She hasn't actually written for ages now. I've written three times in a row.

I would hate to go to boarding school because I'm sure I wouldn't fit in. You have to play team games and I'd never get picked. The teachers would doubt-less make squashing remarks and all the girls would gang up on me.

But if I went to *Miranda's* boarding school she'd look out for me. She's got a new best friend now, I know, but maybe I could be her *old* best friend? Perhaps boarding school wouldn't be quite so bad?

'Can I go to Miranda's boarding school, Dad?' I asked as he got to the bottom of the stairs.

He stopped and stared up at me.

'What?' He seemed to have forgotten what we were talking about. He often does that nowadays.

'Can I go to Miranda's boarding school?' I repeated. My voice sounded funny. I get a little bit scared talking to Dad now even though he's my favourite person in all the world. It's because he can suddenly get so grumpy, growling at me like he *hates* me.

He growled this time.

'For God's sake!' he exploded. He didn't quite say that. He said something much worse. 'Do you think I'm made of money? Do you know how much that flipping boarding school costs per term?' He didn't say 'flipping' either. 'If you want to go to that school then there's no point asking me. Ask your *mother*.'

'I don't want to, Dad, not really. It was just you said I might be going to a new school—' I was getting all worked up, tears spilling down my cheeks.

Dad used to cuddle me when I cried and mop me with his big hanky and call me his little Weepy Winnie. But now he just sighed irritably.

'Don't turn on the waterworks, India. You're not a baby. Forget the school. You'll probably be fine. Oh, do *stop* it. I'm the one who should be blooming crying.' Or words to that effect.

Dad stalked off, leaving me snivelling on the stairs.

I don't know what he's on about. I hate the way he's started to be so horrid to me. Mum's *always* been horrid, even though she's all smiley-smiley sweet talk.

I decided to show them both. I went upstairs with this diary – right upstairs, to the ladder leading to the attic. I climbed up the ladder quick, opened the trap-door, felt around for the light switch, and then shut the trapdoor after me.

It was like my own Anne Frank secret annexe.

Well, not exactly. It was just our attic with the water tank and heaps of clothes and old furniture and trunks and boxes of books. I'd been up there a couple of times with Dad when we first moved here. Dad said he might turn it into a special playroom for me, but he's never got round to it. Mum uses it now to store her old Moya stock.

I flicked through the silly skimpy little tops and trousers, holding them up and pulling faces. I scrumpled the tiniest, tightest dress into a little ball and then kicked it into the corner of the loft. I stuffed several others at the back of an old chair to make a cushion and then I sat down heartily, bouncing up and down for a bit. Then I curled my legs up and wrote my diary.

I wrote and wrote and wrote.

Then I listened.

I was waiting. Waiting for Wanda to start calling for me. Then Mum. Then Dad.

If my rumbling tummy was anything to go by it was way past supper time. I wished I'd thought to bring some kind of provisions with me. I thought of the Mars Bars hidden under my pillow and my mouth watered so much I nearly dribbled.

I wrote some more.

I waited.

I wondered if I simply couldn't hear the outcry downstairs. I lay down and stuck my ear to the crack of the trapdoor. I could just make out a very distant buzz of television and a sudden small swoosh of a tap in the kitchen. Why were they placidly watching television and making coffee? Why weren't they running all over the house calling for me?

Eventually I heard the *slap-shuffle, slap-shuffle* of Wanda's silly teddy-bear slippers. She was obviously starting to search for me.

No, she wasn't. She went into the bathroom and ran a bath. I had been missing for hours and hours and hours. I could have been butchered by a burglar, raped by a robber, abducted by aliens . . . Wanda obviously didn't give a fig. I'd totally disappeared but she wasn't going to let it spoil her long, hot soak in the bath.

What about Mum and Dad? I know I'm a huge disappointment to my Mum – huge being the operative word – but Dad's always said I'm his special girl, the icing on his cake, the jam in his doughnut, the cream in his éclair. The cakes have gone stale now. Dad didn't notice I'd gone missing. No-one did.

When I was absolutely faint with hunger I opened up the trapdoor and clambered down the stairs. I stood there on the landing, feeling as if I'd returned from another dimension. I found Wanda in her room, still very pink from her long bath, her hair hanging like seaweed. She was eating a Mars bar, plugged into her Walkman. She jumped when she saw me.

'Why aren't you looking all over for me?' I demanded.

Wanda blinked at me.

'I don't need to look for you. You're here!' she said, taking another bite of Mars bar.

'Where did you get that Mars bar?' I said. 'Hey, you didn't nick it from under my pillow, did you?'

'You're not allowed to eat Mars bars, your mother says,' said Wanda, munching.

'You pig!' I tried to snatch the Mars bar stub from her but she shoved it in her mouth sharpish. I felt tears stinging my eyes.

'Don't cry, silly. I'll buy you another tomorrow,' said Wanda.

I flounced off. They were tears of frustration and despair, but Wanda would never understand.

I went downstairs. Mum was pacing up and down the hall, jabbering into the phone.

'Look, this is *serious*. I don't care what time it is! You jolly well listen to me!' she declared. 'God, I'm going out of my mind!'

But she wasn't going out of her mind because I'd gone missing. It was just some crisis about her stupid *clothes*.

'That last batch of T-shirts is *entirely* the wrong shade of purple. I wanted *deep* purple, practically blackberry, and these are almost *lilac*, too twee for words—' She put her hand over the phone and cocked her head on one side enquiringly.

'Yes, darling?' she mouthed.

She obviously hadn't noticed I was missing. I could probably disappear for months and remain low on her list of priorities, *way* below lilac T-shirts that should be blackberry.

Dad hadn't noticed either. He was slumped in front of the television watching *Who Wants to be a Millionaire?* He didn't even look up when I went into the room.

I don't think I love him any more.

I don't love *anyone*.

Oh, dear Kitty, dear Kitty, I wish you were real.

Five

Treasure

I do love it at my nan's. I'm really, truly staying for ever. I've even started school here!

I *did* wonder if it was just a holiday visit in spite of Nan's reassurances. She asked me on New Year's Day if I was missing my mum. I said, 'No, not at all.' It isn't *exactly* true. I dream about her every night. Terry's in the dream too and he's hitting her and I can't stop him and then he's hitting me. Sometimes I'm screaming when I wake up.

I think about Mum during the day too, especially when I make Nan a cup of tea. I settle her down while she's sipping, slip her high heels off and give her a foot massage. That's what I always did to give Mum a little treat. I am the bee's knees at foot massage. I know how to pull the tights gently at the end so the toes can wriggle around. I stroke each toe individually and then spend ages on the instep because that's the bit where it really aches. Nan makes exactly the same little purring sounds that Mum does.

I think about Mum in the evenings too. Terry's always out at the pub then, so why doesn't she phone me? I got so scared he'd really gone for her, maybe put her in hospital. I waited until Nan was out giving a dancing lesson and then I phoned home.

My fingers were so dithery I could hardly tap out the number. I heard the phone ringing and ringing. I closed my eyes tight, the blood beating in my eyelids. Then Mum suddenly said, 'Hello?' right in my ear. She sounded bright and bouncy, like she didn't have a care in the world. She didn't sound like she was missing me one bit.

I swallowed, trying to get my mouth wet enough to speak. I heard Bethany in the background say, 'Who is it, Mum?' It was like a punch in the stomach. I'm sure Bethany never called her 'Mum' before. I slammed the phone down quick without saying a word.

I waited. She didn't dial 1471. She didn't ring back.

I'm not going to ring her again. There's no point now I know she's all right. She's got Bethany and Kyle to watch out for her. Terry won't turn on them because he's their dad. So it's all worked out wonderfully well. *It has. It has. It has.*

When Nan came home all hot and happy from her dancing I put my arms tight round her neck.

'Promise I can stay here for ever, Nan?'

She laughed. 'Yes, I promise! How many more times, my little Treasure?'

She picked me up and I wound my legs tight round her waist as if I was baby Britney. Nan whirled me round and round the living room, going, 'My little Treasure, my gold rings, my silver bangles, my flashy diamond, my sparkly sapphire, my red ruby.'

Patsy capered by her side, doing a little Irish jig, her skirt flying up to show her frilly knickers.

I can fit into Patsy's school uniform – just. Nan's going to buy me my own skirt and blouse soon, *and* some out-of-school clothes too, new trousers and tops and a winter coat because I've only got my old brown fleece and it's so rubbed I look like a jumble-sale teddy. But I'll have to wait a bit because she's already had to fork out for my wonderful new designer glasses so she's a bit strapped for cash at the moment.

I felt strange when Nan took me to the school. Patsy's blouse is very tight under my armpits and her pleated skirt shows a lot of my skinny legs. Patsy's only got one school jumper so I wore one of Willie's even though it's way too big. I spent ages puffing out my fringe so that the Terry scar didn't show. The stitches are out now but it still looks a horrible zig-zag mess. Nan watched me combing and looked like she might be going to cry.

'I've a good mind to shop that pig to the police after all,' she said.

'Don't, Nan! He'll only take it out on Mum.'

'Not if he's put behind bars where he belongs.' Nan shook her head. 'It's so *swearword swearword* ironic!'

She closed her eyes tight for a moment to keep the tears in. I patted her gently on her shoulder. Nan's boyfriend Pete – Patsy's dad – *is* behind bars. He's a really lovely, kind man. Even Willie and Loretta think the world of him. Nan's nuts about him. He's crazy about her too. That's how he got into trouble. He got involved in this fight in a bar, getting stuck in to protect my nan because some drunk guy started chatting her up. Pete was holding his glass in his hand and the drunk guy got cut really badly. So badly that he died, so Pete's doing time for manslaughter. Nan goes to visit him every month. She's got half a gold heart locket that she wears round her neck. Pete wears the other half. It's dead romantic. Nan misses him very, very badly but she keeps it all inside most of the time.

I told her she should have a good weep if she wanted as it would do her good to let her emotions out. Nan roared with laughter instead and said I was a scream. At least it cheered her up a bit.

We went off to school, Nan and Patsy and me. Willie goes to the comprehensive and Loretta doesn't go to school at all now she's got Britney. I felt a bit shy when we went into the playground, especially as all Patsy's friends were crowding round and everyone was wondering who I was. The weird kid with the wrong-size clothes.

'This is my Treasure,' said Nan, like she was really proud of me.

That made me feel great, even though some of the kids sniggered at my name. Nan led me inside the school. Patsy gave me a quick kiss for good luck. Then I was taken to the headteacher, Mrs Parker.

'This is my granddaughter, Treasure. She's living with me now,' said Nan, giving my shoulder a squeeze. 'I've come to enrol her at Latimer.'

I thought I might have to do a test, English and Maths maybe, but Mrs Parker put my name on the register right away and I was given a class. They all stared at me when I walked in. I stared right back, my eyes swivelling round and round. I always look out for someone to be my special friend but I haven't found her yet. The kids at the top of the class with shiny hair and tidy uniform always edge away, like they'll be nibbled by nits if they get near me. The scruffy kids with stains all over their sweatshirts can't stick me either because I'm swotty and they act like they're stupid.

Sometimes the teachers like me. Sometimes they don't. They called me Miss-Know-It-All at my last school. I heard them discussing me in the staffroom. This new teacher Miss Strand is a bit dubious. She thinks I'm thick. She tells me stuff very s-l-o-w-l-y and she keeps saying I mustn't worry if I can't do the work. It's a wonder she hasn't stuck me at the back with a colouring book like the kids with learning difficulties.

She had problems with my name too, her lip curling every time she said it, like she was trying not to laugh. The kids are a pain about it too. I have a new nickname, not in the least original. *Buried*.

'You think *you've* got problems with your name, Treasure,' said Willie when we were having tea. 'What kind of a nut calls their son "Willie"?'

'A *hard* nut, so less of the cheek,' said Nan, pretending to bop him one. 'Did those kids really give you a rough time, Treasure?'

'No, no worries, Nan, I'm used to it. It's always like this when I start at a new school,' I said, wolfing down my egg and bacon and sausage and tomatoes and mushrooms and chips. I can't get over how wonderful the food is at Nan's. She cooks it all herself – no running down to the chippie for *her*. She's teaching me to cook too. I was the sausage girl tonight and Nan said they were perfect, well done but not the slightest bit burnt.

'How many schools have you been to, Treasure?' Nan asked.

'Oh goodness, I don't know, Nan. Heaps,' I said.

Mum's lived all over the place with all different blokes. Each time she gets a new guy there's a new home and a new school. It's awful always being the new girl and never remembering all the names of everyone in my new class. I get to know the girls who start picking on me first. It's never the boys, they leave me alone, but there's nearly always a little group of girls who corner me in the cloakrooms, shove me in the corridors, trip me in the playground.

It's OK. I can cope. I might be puny but I'm POWERFUL. I'm not too great at punching but I can give a hard whack if necessary. I mostly just say stuff. I give them a verbal version of the Terry Tortures and they reel backwards. Sometimes they cry, even the really mean tough ones. Then they leave me alone. But that's OK too. It *is*. I like my own company.

School doesn't matter that much anyway. It's home that counts. I get up really, really early sometimes, when everyone else is still asleep, even little Britney. I pad softly round the house in my bare feet, so happy that it's my home and I live here. I stroke the smooth leather sofa in the living room, I rub my cheek on the gold velvet cushions, I curl up my toes in the black and white furry rug, and I run my finger up and down the big yellow lava lamp. I love that lamp and the slow, sure, steady way the oil wafts up and down.

I peep in at everyone while they're asleep. My family. Patsy always curls up in a neat little ball with a blue rabbit on one side and a squat koala on the other. I like it that she's got her cuddly toys. She doesn't really *play* with them though. She hasn't even given them proper names – they are just Bunny and Bear. It's a wonder Patsy doesn't call me 'Girl'.

Willie doesn't sleep curled up and he certainly doesn't have any cuddly toys. He lies flat on his back with his arms flung out and his feet sticking out of the duvet. There's always a fug of old sock in his room so I don't linger long. He'd go berserk if he knew I'd been peeping at him. One time he'd kicked his duvet right off and I saw him in his underpants!

Loretta sometimes sleeps in her underwear too, but

she's got pretty slinky petticoats so she looks fine, though she's always got black circles from her eye make-up which spoils the effect a bit. Britney sleeps in a cot at the end of her bed. She wears dear little yellow towelling suits with a yellow dummy to match. She makes little sucking sounds every now and then. She's so sweet.

I often tiptoe into the kitchen and make up her bottle for when she wakes, around six. Then I make a cup of tea and take it into Nan. She looks so lovely when she's in bed. Her long blond hair spreads out all over the pillow and she wears fancy black lacy nighties so she looks just like a film star, even though her face has got a few wrinkles.

'My laughter lines,' says Nan. It's true, she's always laughing. It makes you feel so good, so safe, so happy. When I wake her she never yells at me or pushes me away. She smiles like she's really pleased to see me.

'Hello, my little Treasure,' she says.

She props herself up on her pink pillow to sip her tea. I slip in beside her and cuddle up close. I can't understand my mum. Why did she ever want to leave home? Why did she go off with all the horrible boyfriends? She didn't even know my dad properly, so I can't get to know him myself. Not that I care. I haven't liked any of my step-dads so I expect my real dad is just as bad. And Terry is the WORST ever.

I *wish* I could stop dreaming that he's coming to get me.

Six

India

Dear Kitty

I hate school. I hate all the teachers. I hate all the girls. I particularly hate Maria and Alice.

They raise their eyebrows and then sputter with laughter whenever I go near them. The other girls have started doing it too. And everyone groans whenever I answer in class. I can't *help* knowing lots. What's so *bad* about being clever?

I wish I didn't have to go to school. Maybe I'll bunk off and creep back home and hide in the attic all day like a real Anne Frank.

I got into trouble because of my darling Anne today. I was so excited because we're doing Diaries in English and Mrs Gibbs started talking about Anne

Frank. She read out an excerpt from the diary. I felt my face flushing as if she were reading out *my* diary. I couldn't stand it that some of the girls were just messing around and not paying attention when they were being introduced to the most important book of the twentieth century. It is so insulting to Anne. I couldn't bear it.

Mrs Gibbs read on, her voice solemn and portentous, *sooooo* wrong for lively, passionate Anne. Some of the girls started *giggling* while I fidgeted miserably to try to distract myself from the Gibbs rendition. I ended up slumped right down in my desk, my hands over my ears.

'India?'

I jumped. I'd filtered out her voice a little too effectively.

'What's the matter with you? Aren't you even listening?' Mrs Gibbs gave me a wounded look. 'I would have thought you of all people would be interested in Anne Frank.'

'I *am*.'

'Then please sit up properly and concentrate.'

Mrs Gibbs trudged on through Anne's delicate prose, selecting the passage which means most to me, the one where Anne desperately longs for a real friend. I listened in agony. Alice whispered some crass remark and Maria spluttered infuriatingly.

'Really, girls!' said Mrs Gibbs, closing Anne's diary with a snap. 'Can't you be a little more mature? Maria, it's not funny.'

'I'm sorry, Mrs Gibbs,' said Maria, struggling. 'So what happened to Anne Frank? Did she stay hidden in her secret annexe till the war ended?'

Mrs Gibbs adjusted her glasses, rubbing the lenses with the bottom of her cardigan. Her eyes looked horribly pink and naked without them.

'I'm afraid Anne's story has a sad ending. Her family were caught and sent away to a concentration camp.'

'*This* is like a concentration camp,' Alice hissed.

Maria giggled.

I stood up, cheeks flaming. 'How can you be so *stupid*?' I shouted.

'India!' said Mrs Gibbs.

They were all staring at me. I was living up to my red hair at last. I felt as if I was on fire.

'The concentration camps were the most terrible places ever. Haven't you heard of the gas chambers? Nearly everyone *died* there. You were sent in cattle trucks, stuck in the dark for days. People often died on the journey. When you got there they divided up all the families. Anne wasn't allowed to stay with her father. And you were stripped naked and—'

'That's enough, India,' said Mrs Gibbs.

'And your head was shaved and then you were kept in terrible, squalid, freezing old huts with hardly any food at all, just rotten scraps, and so everyone got terrible illnesses. Anne's mother died and then her sister Margot died and so poor Anne was all on her own. And she got typhoid too and then *she* died, in agony—'

'*India!*' Mrs Gibbs got hold of me by the shoulders and pushed me down in my seat. 'Will you be quiet!'

'But it's true!'

'I know it is. But I don't think we should dwell on things in quite such a ghoulish way. You're upsetting the other girls.'

'But we *should* feel upset. Anne died. Six *million* Jews died.'

'Yes, I know. It was terrible. But it was a long time ago. It's silly to cry about it now.'

I wiped my eyes fiercely with the back of my hand. I stuck my chin out to show I wasn't one little bit ashamed of crying. Mrs Gibbs sighed and then carried on with the lesson. She stopped talking about Anne. She moved hastily on to Samuel Pepys.

When the bell went for hometime she called me back to have a word with her.

'I'm sorry you got so upset in class, India,' she said. 'I'm very impressed that you know so much about Anne Frank. You've obviously been very moved by her story. But I can't have you shouting like that in the classroom.'

'But the others were being so stupid. They were laughing and messing about.'

'I know, India. It's very annoying. But you mustn't *mind* so much. You feel things so intensely, dear. It's a little unnerving.'

I don't think I feel too much. I think other people don't feel enough. But I know this is the reason most people don't like me. It's not just Maria and Alice. All the other girls think I'm odd. Even Miranda, who really did use to be my best friend, frequently declared I was seriously weird. Mum is always sighing and telling me not to be such a drama queen. Wanda tells me to lighten up. Dad used to pick me up and shake me until I squealed – it was a game to shake all my worries away. We haven't played that for ages. Maybe it's because I've got too big. Or maybe even Dad doesn't like me any more.

I started crying again in front of Mrs Gibbs. I was remembering another game Dad used to play. He would curl his fingers into a spanner shape and gently touch my eyelids, making little wrenching sounds. 'We'd better fix the washer on this funny little tear tap,' he'd say and it would make me stop crying and laugh instead.

It's as if that Dad has left home and a grumpy stranger has moved into his body.

'What is it *now*, India?' said Mrs Gibbs. 'Come on, try not to be such a baby. I'm not telling you off, I'm just trying to have a little chat with you.'

'I know,' I mumbled, sniffing.

'Haven't you got a hanky, dear? India . . . things are all right at home, aren't they?'

I jumped.

'You know you can always talk to me, don't you? Is there anything really worrying you?'

I clicked on various images in my mind: Dad, Mum, Wanda. I scrolled down each long list of worries. I couldn't decide which to highlight. The Dad Dilemma was in the boldest font but I didn't want to tell Mrs Gibbs about him. He's still the most special person in all the world to me (apart from Anne). It would seem horribly disloyal if I started whining about him.

I didn't mind whining about *Mum* but this is a non-starter. Mrs Gibbs reveres her. She's always going on about her success and her stupid, simpering appearances on breakfast television. (Mum was even on *Blue Peter* once – with Phoebe.) I wondered about telling Mrs Gibbs what Mum's *really* like, but it's hard to put into words, even if you're 'extremely articulate, perhaps a little precociously so'. That was Mrs Gibbs's comment on my school report at Christmas.

Mum doesn't do anything bad to me. She doesn't *say* anything either. It's the way she says it. The way she sighs. The way she raises her eyebrows. The way she rushes straight past me, talking over her shoulder. The way she never wants to sit down and talk to me. If I try to grab hold of her and start gabbling she always goes, 'Oh darling, I'm in such a tearing rush. Can't you ask Wanda?'

Wanda's no use whatever. Especially recently. She just stays in her room most of the time. She doesn't even go out with Suzi any more. I don't think they're friends now. Wanda hasn't got any other friends. *I'd* be her friend but she barely takes any notice of me.

I wondered about having a good moan to Mrs Gibbs about Wanda but I couldn't be bothered. Besides, Mrs Gibbs might have a word with Mum and then Wanda would get into trouble. Then *I'd* be for it. Wanda's got these pointy long nails and it really hurts when she pinches.

'No, everything's fine at home, really,' I said, sighing.

Mrs Gibbs sighed too and told me to perk up then, as if I was a jug of coffee. The cloakroom was empty when I got my coat. Everyone had gone home already. I trailed out across the playground, expecting Wanda to nag at me for keeping her waiting. But Wanda wasn't there. She wasn't standing by the gate, leaning on the wall, wandering up and down the pavement. I looked for the car but it wasn't parked anywhere.

I wondered if Wanda had nipped along to the corner shop for some chocolate. I went to have a look. She wasn't there either. I bought myself a Mars bar – king size – and ate it in five gollops while I wondered what to do.

I could go back to school and tell Mrs Gibbs.

I could find a phone box and ring home.

I could ring for a taxi.

I could stand outside the school waiting and waiting and waiting.

I could walk home by myself. I thought about it. I knew the way. It wasn't *that* far. It would only take twenty minutes, half an hour at the most. So I set off, my school bag bumping on my back. It felt as if I was starting out on an adventure. I enjoyed the feeling. Maybe I wouldn't go home. Maybe I'd walk off into the wide world and seek my fortune. No, I didn't want to sound like a fairy tale. I wanted to be part of a stark modern drama. I played a tragic runaway picked up by a wicked man who kept me captive and forced me to submit to his evil intentions . . .

'Wait a minute, little girl!' A fat man suddenly grabbed hold of me. I gave a little squeak of terror.

'You nearly walked right out into the road!' he puffed, his sausage fingers still splayed on my shoulders. 'You could have stepped straight under a lorry. You were in a right old daydream.'

'I'm sorry,' I stammered and rushed off – in the wrong direction. I felt such a fool I kept on running. I looked round quickly as I turned the corner, just to make sure he wasn't following me. He wasn't the wicked man of my fantasy, just a kind grandad in a too-tight bomber jacket trying to stop me getting run over, but I felt I couldn't be too careful.

I couldn't see him but I didn't want to retrace my footsteps just in case he bobbed back again. I'd have to trail right into town and go the really long way home – unless of course I took a short cut through the Latimer Estate.

I did a local history project last year and found out that the Latimer Estate *used* to be Latimer Woods, and all this woodland belonged to the big manor house, Parkfield. Only all the woods got chopped down and built on in Victorian times, and then in the sixties all the little Victorian back-to-backs got pulled down and they built this vast tower-block council estate. Parkfield Manor got pulled down too and they built all *our* houses. We don't get called an estate, we're a 'luxury complex'.

The Latimer Estate is very big, very bleak and very tough. I'd never actually walked through it but we drive past sometimes. Mum always winds up the windows and locks the car door from inside in case any of the Latimer Estate kids charge up at the traffic lights, stick their hands through the window and try to grab her Rolex watch. It's only an imitation one she got in Hong Kong when she went there on a business trip, but it looks real.

No-one's ever *tried* to steal her watch. The only time anyone's approached the car it was to wash the windows and even then they backed off quick when Dad flipped his hands and mouthed at them. But Mum and Dad talk about the Latimer Estate as if it's a suburb of hell itself.

'It's all feckless single mums on drugs and gangs of yobs,' says Mum.

'Drunks and drop-outs the lot of them. I don't know why they don't round them all up and shove them in jail,' says Dad.

Whenever we hear a police siren scream in the distance they sigh and shake their heads and say, 'The Latimer Estate!'

I hate it when they talk like that.

My feet hurt in my hard school shoes and my bag was dragging on my shoulder. I didn't want to trail all the way into town. I decided to be daring. I'd walk through the Latimer Estate all by myself.

I set off, feeling like Little Red Riding Hood setting off into deep, dark Latimer Woods. I walked very briskly in spite of my sore feet, almost as if real wolves were after me. Two old ladies hauling shopping trollies and three mums with baby buggies wheeling washing back from the launderette didn't look too scary, but as I got further into the estate, the stained concrete tower blocks high above my head, I started to feel more wary.

Something wet spattered on top of my head. It wasn't raining. I put my hand up gingerly to feel what it was. I heard a faraway giggle from one of the balconies. I was obviously a target in a spitting competition.

I hurried on, looking up worriedly every so often. It was bad enough being spat at. What if they started chucking things at me? Weren't they meant to have thrown an old television at a policeman only the other day? My own prissy private-school uniform was reason enough for them to have a go at me.

I huddled inside my duffel coat and walked on as fast as I could.

'Wibble wobble, jelly bum!'

It was a sharp-faced little kid about six shouting at me from the dustbin shelter. I tossed my head, ignoring him. He started yelling worse things, swear words I'd never heard said aloud before.

'Wash your mouth out with soap!' I said. My voice sounded horribly posh and plummy. He screamed with laughter.

I hurried on to the next block. There were bigger boys there, swooping round and round on skateboards, thundering up a home-made chute, flying through the air and then crashing down on the asphalt. I jumped each time they thumped, scuttling between them as they circled me.

There was a girl cycling round and round too, doing fantastic wheelie tricks on a BMX. She looked every bit as tough as the boys, her hair tousled, a big red scar on her forehead, her face pale and pinched. She was so skinny in her tight jeans and tiny matted fleece. I stared at her enviously.

She saw me staring. She stuck her tongue out at me.

I waggled mine back at her.

Then she grinned. I grinned. It was just as if we knew each other.

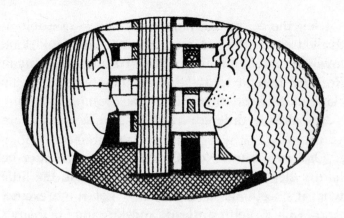

Seven

Treasure

Mum rang. Out of the blue.

'Hi, Treasure,' she said casually, as if I'd just popped round to Nan's for tea.

'Mum!' My mouth was so dry I could hardly speak.

'What's up with your voice, Treasure? You got a cold? Typical! I bet you haven't been wearing your fleece.'

Mum's voice sounded so *normal*. It made it easier.

'I'm fine, Mum. Honest. And Nan's getting me a new coat out of her catalogue. A red one. It's lovely.'

'You can't wear red, you're far too pale. It sucks all the colour out of your cheeks. Tell your nan not to waste her money. There's plenty of wear in that fleece of yours.'

I felt the colour rushing *to* my cheeks. I'd felt so thrilled about the red coat. Nan said it would look lovely on me. Willie teased me a bit and sang *Lady in Red* and Loretta said she liked the style and Patsy clapped her hands and said I'd look *beautiful*.

'It's already ordered, Mum,' I said. 'Anyway, are you . . . OK?'

'Of course I am. Well, Gary is driving me nuts, he hardly slept a wink last night, but I think the little whatsit's teething so maybe he's got some excuse. And Kyle's getting dead cheeky and Bethany's forever complaining, the stroppy little cow, but that's nothing new. She says she's missing you, babe. Sweet, eh, when you two were always driving me daft with your fights. Still, we're all missing you, Treasure.'

My throat closed up.

'I miss you too, Mum,' I croaked.

'So when are you coming back? Shall we come and fetch you on Saturday?'

Nan's bright room suddenly broke up into tiny pieces in front of my eyes. Kaleidescope patterns whirled round even when I shut my eyes.

'I'm not coming back, Mum,' I whispered.

'You what? Do speak up, babe, I've got Gary yelling in his kiddie-chair, can't you hear him? I think he's missing you too. You're like a little mother to him. You're always very good with the kids.'

'Mum, listen. I live with Nan now. You know I do. It was all fixed after Terry . . . you know.'

'What, after that little set-to? Look, that got blown up out of all proportion. You know it was a complete accident. Terry didn't mean to hit you. It was just a little nick anyway, nothing to get worked up about.'

I fingered the long raised scar underneath my fringe.

'And you were a very naughty girl, writing all that rude childish stuff about him. No wonder he got angry. But he's willing to let bygones be bygones. He's been a changed guy since, anyway. He's hardly touched a drop of whisky. He's sticking to his beer and that never makes him mean. He's been really sweet to me and the kids. It's a fresh start, Treasure. You've no worries on that score.'

'Mum, I want to stay *here*. With Nan.'

Mum's tone changed. 'Well, you can't! *I'm* your mum, and *I* look after you. I need you back here, sharpish. I let you stay with your nan over the holidays for a little break, but it's not like it's *permanent*. School's started now, you have to come back. They've been on at me, wondering where you are.'

'I go to school here now, Mum. Up Latimer.'

'You what? You can't swap schools just like that! The nerve of it. You're coming home this weekend, do you hear me?'

I heard. I put the phone down and wept. Nan had left me alone in the living room so I could talk to Mum privately. She came back to find me curled up crying into a cushion on her sofa.

'Hey, don't get that gold velveteen all snotty, sweet-heart,' she said, lifting me up and putting her arms tight round me. 'Now, tell Nan. What's your mum said?'

'Oh Nan, I've got to go home!'

'Do you want to?'

'No!'

'Well then, it's simple. You're not going.'

'But Mum says—'

'I'm *her* mum and *I* say you're staying,' Nan said firmly. 'I'll phone her right back and tell her straight.'

She did too. There was one BIG row over the phone. My mum said she was still coming. With Terry.

'Like that's going to frighten me, Tammy,' said Nan. 'That bloke of yours might get off on cutting up little girls like Treasure but I don't think he's got the bottle to take *me* on.'

She's right too. Nan can get the better of anyone.

I know I can trust Nan. But I still feel a bit jumpy.

I couldn't sleep last night so Nan let me cuddle up in her bed. Then Patsy came in too so it got a bit crowded but Nan didn't mind a bit.

'I've got two arms for my two girls,' she said, and she cuddled us both.

Then when I got back from school today Willie said I could have a go on his bike as he was off round a mate's house to play computer games. I was dead chuffed because Willie's bike is seriously wicked and he won't let Patsy so much as *touch* it.

I used to beg to go on Kyle's bike back home – no,

back *then*, *this* is home – so I know what I'm doing. I raced it round and round the grounds. The boys wouldn't let me on their ramp so I couldn't try out any really daredevil stuff but I stuck my head in the air like I didn't care and did neat bunny-hops and perfect 360s just to show them I was no toddler on its first trike.

They pretended they weren't watching, but they *were*. There was this other girl too, dead posh, in one of those weird old-fashioned uniforms like she'd stepped straight out of some 1950s time-warp. She even had long socks and button-over shoes like babies wear. She looked like she'd talk all toffee-nosed but she didn't seem snooty. She was staring at me, but it was like she thought I was special.

I rode round and her head swivelled, her beady brown eyes fixed on me. I stuck my tongue out at her. I wondered if she'd look shocked but she stuck her tongue out back at me, as if it was our own secret signal.

I *liked* her.

I wondered what on earth she was doing on our estate. I watched her walk off. Then I started pedalling like crazy after her. She dodged when she heard me coming, like she thought I was trying to slam straight into her. I braked and leapt off, landing on my toes, dead cool.

'Hiya!'

'Hi,' she said.

Her voice was horribly high and plummy. She licked her lips nervously. I could tell it worried her too.

71

'What's your name then?'

This *really* got her. Lick, lick, lick with her little pointy tongue.

'India.'

'What? Like the place?'

'Yes. It's a stupid name.' She went very pink.

'I like place names. Like Brooklyn for a boy. Is that where your mum and dad started you?'

'I don't know. Maybe.' She pulled a face.

I giggled. 'Yeah, isn't it weird, thinking of them doing it? I'm glad my mum didn't call me after a place. I'd be Staines!'

I leant Willie's bike against the wall and swung myself up on it. India joined me, though she had to have several goes heaving herself up. We sat dangling our legs, nodding at each other.

'So what's your name?'

'It's heaps more stupid than yours. Treasure.'

'That's your nickname?'

'No, my *real* name.'

'Well . . . it's obvious your mum thought a lot of you when you were born.'

She'd got this *sooooo* wrong.

'I'm changing it when I'm older. I like Tiffany. Or Yasmin. Or a jewel name like Amber or Jade or Ruby.'

'I want to change my name too. I want to be called Anne. You know, after Anne Frank.'

'Cool,' I said, though I don't know who Anne Frank is. Someone on television?

'She's my heroine,' said India. 'Who's yours?'

I shrugged. Then I knew. 'My nan.'

'Your nan?'

It did sound strange said in India's posh voice but she wasn't going to faze me.

'She's fantastic, my nan. You ask anyone on the estate about Rita. She's like their queen. I live with her now.'

'What about your mother?'

'Oh, she's got this bloke, see, and we don't get on.'

India didn't look as if she did see, but she nodded politely.

'So this is my home now,' I said, waving back at the flats. 'Where do you live, India?'

'Oh, over there,' she said. Her wave was a lot vaguer than mine.

'Not on our estate,' I said. 'You're rich, aren't you?'

She went pink again, playing with a frizzy end of hair.

I suddenly realized. 'Hey, you don't live in those huge great houses where they had the fireworks? Parkfield?'

She nodded, ducking her head like she wanted to disappear inside her duffel coat.

'Wow, you lucky thing! So what are you doing hanging round our estate then?'

'I'm going home from school.'

'How come you aren't being fetched in your Mercedes or your Daimler or whatever?'

'It's just a Range Rover. Wanda didn't turn up.'

'Is that your mum?'

'No, she's . . . she's the au pair.'

'The what?'

'Well, she stays with us and sort of works for us.'

'You mean like a servant?'

'A bit. I don't know what's happened to her. My mum will go spare if she finds out.' India sighed and raised her eyebrows. They were ginger, like her fuzzy hair. 'My mum's this incredible drama queen. She *always* makes a fuss.'

'What about your dad? Is he OK?'

'Oh, he's lovely. Well, he *was* – but he's got ever so grumpy lately. He'll yell at me for the least little thing.'

'Does he whack you one?'

She looked shocked. 'He'd never hit me!' Her eyes went straight to the scar on my forehead.

I nodded. 'Yeah, my mum's bloke did that. With his belt.'

'How awful!'

I shrugged. 'Well, that's Terry for you,' I said, acting like it didn't really worry me.

I still dream about him every night. Nan says I'll forget him soon. Maybe this is the one time Nan's got it wrong.

'This Terry? You said he's your mum's . . . bloke?'

'Yeah, but like I said, that's past history now.'

We nodded. There was a little pause. We looked away. We looked back at each other – and giggled.

'So, you like it here? With your nan?' India says.

'It's great.' I look back at the stained concrete walls

and the black plastic bags spilling rubbish. 'Well, you probably think it's a right dump.'

'No I don't,' she says quickly. 'It's . . . it's very nice. Sort of cosy.'

I whoop with laughter. 'You are a nut, India. Cosy! Look, do you want to come and have some tea and meet my nan?'

'Well . . .' She looked quickly at her little gold watch.

'You've got to get back home, I suppose.'

'Yes. No! There's no-one there apart from Mrs Winslow and Wanda, and goodness knows where she is.'

'Mrs Winslow?'

'She's . . . well, she's the cleaning lady.'

'Wow, you are *so* posh. Hey, you're not Little *Lady* India, are you? Maybe I should curtsey?'

'Shut up! Look, do you mean it? Can I really come for tea?'

'Sure.'

'Your nan won't mind?'

'Don't be so daft, of course she won't. She'll be thrilled in fact. She's worried I haven't made any friends here yet.'

'How long have you been here?'

'Couple of weeks.'

'My goodness, your nan would have a nervous breakdown over me. I've been living in the same house for the last five years and I haven't got any friends. Well, not *real* ones.' She pulled a face. 'Oh gosh, that makes me sound seriously *sad*.'

I burst out laughing.

'Don't laugh at me. I can't help it.'

'I'm laughing at the "Oh gosh" bit. I didn't know people really said stuff like that. I'm not laughing at *you*.' I gave her a friendly dig in the ribs. 'Come on, Nan's flat's in Elm block. I'd give you a ride on the bike back but it's Willie's and he only let *me* go on it as a special favour.'

She hopped and skipped along beside me and then panted up the stairs after me. I'm supposed to use the lift because of my asthma but that didn't seem like a good idea, even though we had to hoick the bike up between us. Boys keep peeing in the lift – or worse.

I was starting to wonder if it was such a good idea inviting India back. Her eyes went round as saucers when she saw what some of the kids had scribbled all over the walls. Then she nearly jumped out of her funny freckled skin when two of Willie's mates came barging downstairs, effing and blinding and waving their cans of lager around for our benefit.

'Get out of our *blankety blank* way, little girlies.'

'You get out of *our blankety blank* way, big *blankety* boys,' I said back, gesturing rudely with my fingers.

I only did it because I *know* them, but India looked dead impressed, like I was the really tough kid on the block.

As we ran along the balcony, me scooting it on Willie's bike, mean old Mrs Watkins banged open her door, nearly knocking me flying. She started yelling about 'you kids' and how someone had smashed her milk bottles the other day and it just wasn't good enough, she was going to report it, *bla bla bla*. Mumbly Michael pulled faces behind her in their hallway. He's her grown-up son but Nan says he's not quite the ticket. I burst out laughing when he crossed his eyes and smacked his lips open and shut in a pretty accurate imitation of his mum. India started giggling too. Mrs Watkins thought we were laughing at her and yelled even louder. Nan came out on the landing.

'My God, Mrs Watkins, you're frightening the life out of everyone – *and* you've woken little Britney up and she's screaming fit to bust. What on earth has happened?'

Mrs Watkins bellowed like a bull. Nan raised her eyebrows, winked at India and me, and beckoned us along the balcony. She whipped us both inside the flat, shutting the door on Mrs Watkins' wails.

'Daft old bag,' Nan said, shaking her head. 'Don't take any notice, Treasure, she always carries on like that. And who are you, sweetie?' Nan put her hands on India's shoulders, gazing at her with delight. 'Don't you look wonderful! What a fantastic uniform. Is that the Girls' High School?'

India nodded shyly.

'Thought so! What's your name, poppet?'

'India,' she mumbled.

'Oh, stylish,' said Nan. 'I'm Rita, pet, but you can call me Nan. All the kids do.'

'But you're *really* my nan, aren't you?' I said proudly.

'You bet, Treasure,' said Nan, giving me a hug. 'Now, darlings, are you peckish? Come in the kitchen.'

Loretta was boiling the kettle for Britney's bottle. Britney threshed about in her baby-chair, desperate to be fed right now, this minute. Patsy was waving a rattle at her ineffectually.

'Here, baby, come to Treasure,' I said, unstrapping her.

I picked her up and then held her at arm's length, pretending to be cross.

'Oh, that's a nice way to say hello! Pee all over the place, right? We'd better get you changed before we give you to India for a cuddle.'

'India?' said Patsy. 'Cool name. What's it like at your school then? I might be going to this special stage school and they've got dead posh uniform too. Can I try your funny coat on, eh?'

I whipped Britney's nappy off and mopped her up while Patsy pranced round in India's duffel coat, even though it was huge on her, the hem trailing on the carpet. India knelt down beside me, gingerly holding Britney's little hand.

'She's so sweet,' she said. 'What's that cream you're putting on her?'

'Zinc and castor oil so she doesn't get a sore bum.'

'You're ever so good with babies.'

'I've had heaps of practice,' I said, pressing a clean nappy on Britney and stuffing her little legs back into her playsuit. 'I used to look after my baby brother

Gary practically full-time, especially when Mum was poorly.'

'Your mum's a waste of space as far as I'm concerned, even though she's my daughter,' said Nan.

I thought about Saturday and my hands started shaking so I couldn't do up Britney's poppers to save my life.

Eight

India

Dearest Kitty

You'll never ever guess what! I have this incredible new best friend, Treasure. She is so lovely – absolutely ice-cream cool and yet *sooooo* kind to me. She just rode up on her bike and started chatting to me like we'd been friends for ever.

I was a bit scared she might be sending me up, but she was truly friendly and invited me back for tea practically straightaway, no big deal at all, she didn't even need to ask her grandma first.

Treasure's grandma looks incredible, long blond curly hair and bright blue eyes and shiny pink lipstick. She was wearing a tight pink top, black trousers and pink high heels when I first met her. She cooked us tea:

egg and bacon and baked beans and tomato and fried bread for Treasure and me, two eggs and four rashers and extra baked beans and tomato and practically a whole fried loaf for Willie, just baked beans and tomato for Patsy because she has to watch her figure for her future showbiz career, just toast for Loretta because she was going out with her girlfriends and she'd have a pizza later, and runny egg and soldiers for little baby Britney.

Nan served up all these different meals without fussing. She just had a bacon sandwich and a cup of tea herself, because she said she didn't like to eat too much before a class. I wondered if she was some kind of teacher, though she certainly doesn't *look* like one. Then she went and got changed. She came back into the kitchen looking AMAZING in this little white flared skirt with a matching fringed bolero trimmed with gold, and white crocodile cowboy boots.

She winked at me. 'I'm just dashing down to Tesco to do my shopping,' she said. Then she roared with laughter. 'Your *face*, sweetheart! No, this is my work outfit. I teach line dancing.'

'Mum's been the South-East area champion two years running,' Patsy said proudly.

'Patsy's won all sorts of trophies and medals and stuff too, and Loretta used to dance and all, before she had Britney. And Willie's brilliant at disco dancing. I'm the only one who's got two left feet,' said Treasure.

'I'm useless at dancing. I hate school discos, I never know what to do,' I said.

I hate the clothes you're supposed to wear too. Moya Upton clothes.

I *loved* it that Treasure and all her family liked my school uniform. Mum always winces whenever she sees it. Maybe it's just the way I look in it.

I know just what Mum would say about Treasure's grandma in her cowboy clothes. Still *I* think she looked lovely, and she smelled lovely too, all powdery and perfume. She kissed everyone goodbye, even me.

'You come round any time you fancy, India, my lovie,' she said. 'And you're welcome to stay as long as you like, but I think you'd better phone home first, just to let your mum know where you are.'

She offered me her mobile. It had its own little white and gold cover to match her outfit. I said truthfully that my mum wouldn't be home herself. Still, it looked like it was time for me to go. And I had to find out what on earth had happened to Wanda.

She was home – and in tears. She leapt at me the minute I let myself in the front door.

'Where have you *been*, India? I didn't know what to do. I've driven round and round looking for you. I've phoned your dad. He's on his way back from work.'

'You didn't phone Mum, did you?'

'Not yet. I was wondering if I ought to have phoned the *police*. I was sure you'd gone missing.'

'*You* were the one who went missing,' I insisted, staring her straight in the eyes. She'd been crying so much her eyes were pink, like a white rabbit. Did she care about me that much?

82

'What do you mean?' she said, flustered.

'You weren't there when I came out of school. I waited and waited.'

'I was there the usual time. Well, I might have been a *minute* late. The traffic was really bad.'

'A minute! Do you think I'm daft, Wanda? I've got a watch. I waited *fifteen* minutes.'

'Don't tell your father that, please!' Wanda begged.

She didn't really mind about me one bit. She was just scared she was going to get into trouble and maybe lose her job.

'It's true though, isn't it?' I said.

'Maybe I was five minutes late – but I'm sure it couldn't have been more than that. I fell asleep. I wasn't even on my bed, I was sitting at the kitchen table and I just nodded off. Mrs Winslow just *left* me there. Can you imagine anyone so mean? She just doesn't like me. No-one likes me.'

Wanda started crying again. I couldn't help feeling sorry for her. I put my arms round her.

'Don't cry, Wanda. It's OK. Look, *I* like you.'

'Your mother hates me. She said the most terrible things to me last night. She says I'm totally useless—'

'She thinks I'm useless too, she thinks everyone is. Never mind her. Look, my dad likes you.'

'Does he? Does he *really*? What has he said?'

Wanda was suddenly peering eagerly at me out of her long dark hair, tears still rolling down her cheeks. I felt hurt. She didn't seem to care one way or the other when I said *I* liked her.

I took my arms away. 'Oh, I don't know. I'm not sure he's actually *said* anything – but of course he likes you.' She looked so pathetically pleased I couldn't help adding spitefully, 'He's liked *all* our au pairs.'

That made her droop again.

'But maybe I won't tell him you were at *least* fifteen minutes late,' I said.

Wanda looked hopeful.

'I promise I won't do it to you again, India. I was just so *tired*. I'm not sleeping properly at night. It's awful, I just toss and turn.'

She did look tired out. The dark smudges under her eyes weren't just her eye make-up.

'Yeah, OK, I'll make out I just waited a minute or two, right? Only maybe you can do something for me in return?'

'You mean chocolate? OK,' said Wanda eagerly.

'No, I mean a bit more than chocolate, actually. Look, it's a little bit mad your coming to meet me after school all the time. It's so babyish. And you've got other things to do – like sleep.'

'India, I slept *once*.'

'So why don't we have an arrangement? I'll come home from school by myself. I promise I'll always be home long before Dad or Mum gets back. OK?'

'No, of course it's not OK! What are you up to, India? Where did you go today?'

'Well . . . this odd guy was waiting outside the school and he asked if I wanted to go off and buy some sweets with him—' I burst out laughing at the expression on Wanda's face. *'Joke*, Wanda!'

'You *didn't* go off with any guy?'

'Of course not! No, I went and played round at my friend's place.' The word 'friend' tasted like honey on my tongue.

'You've got a *friend*, India?'

I felt insulted but I needed Wanda on my side so I didn't over-react.

'Tell me all about her,' Wanda said. She fixed me a cup of hot chocolate with extra whipped cream on top. I was still full from Rita's scrummy fry-up but I can't ever resist hot chocolate. Wanda said she didn't fancy one herself, she was feeling a bit queasy. She kept me company while I licked and sipped and told her all about Treasure.

I didn't tell her the *truth* of course. Wanda isn't snobby like Mum and Dad but she might get a bit fussed if she knew I had a friend on the Latimer Estate. I called Treasure by her own favourite name Tiffany and I pretended she was in my class at school. I said she had a fantastic grandma – I turned her into an ex-ballet dancer who now works in the arts. I am very skilled at lying when I want to be.

Wanda is lousy at it. Dad arrived home in a right state but when he saw me he hugged me tight as tight, even picking me up and whirling me round like he did when I was little. It was so great to have him back being *Dad* again. I felt I could whirl right up to the ceiling and revolve around the trendy lily light-fittings all by myself.

85

But then Dad sat me down and turned to Wanda. He asked her why the whatsit she hadn't met me from school. Wanda blushed a painful meat-red and said she'd only been a little bit late, maybe a minute, but it was obvious she was fibbing. I had to butt in quickly and tell Dad it was all my fault – I'd gone dashing off with this new friend of mine and it had been very thoughtless of me and I wouldn't ever worry poor Wanda again.

'Never mind Wanda. You're not to worry *me*, oh Special Exotic Continent,' Dad said – another pet name he hasn't used for *ages*.

Then we had the most beautiful time together, Dad and Wanda and me. We watched children's telly, Dad imitating half the people until we were in stitches. Then Dad said he was peckish and didn't want to wait for dinner so he went out for a pizza – *each!*

Wanda only ate a weeny slice of hers so I ate the rest, gobbling quickly in case Mum came home early and created a drama about my mega-calorie consumption. But she came home even later than usual, long after I'd gone to bed, because there was some boring crisis about her new baby range (the weeniest little brushed denim black-and-white striped dungarees with black sweatshirts and black pull-on booties and little black fleece jackets with hoods. I wanted Mum to give me an outfit for my old teddy Edwina but she raised her eyebrows and sighed as if it was hugely embarrassing having a great lump of a daughter still playing with *teddies* so I didn't pursue it and Edwina's still in her bobbly pink cardi and a droopy yellow dress that clashes with her fur).

It was great that Mum was late because *Dad* came to tuck me up when I went to bed. He was still in his lovely good mood. He gave me a kiss on each ear and one on my nose. He kissed Edwina's one ear and nose too. Then he cuddled us both and said, 'Night night, Sleep tight, Don't let the *bears* bite' and he made Edwina attack me with her little sewn smile.

It's just like the old days. I'm *sooooo* happy. Dad still loves me lots and lots. Wanda and I have our special secret pact. And *I've got a best friend!*

It's *not* like the old days. Something's going on between Dad and Wanda! I woke up early this morning. I heard Mum slamming the front door. She always goes really early, fitting in a jog before work. I lay in bed having a happy doze with Edwina. I heard Wanda going downstairs, her teddy-bear slippers going *slop-slop*. She started talking to Dad down in the kitchen. I couldn't hear a word they were saying but I could tell something was wrong. Wanda's voice went *drone drone drone* and then Dad's voice went *buzz buzz buzz*.

I wondered if Wanda had decided to come clean with Dad and tell him the truth about last night. I shot downstairs in my pyjamas to see if I could salvage the situation. They both jumped when they saw me. Wanda was in *her* pyjamas too, well, her vest-top and shorts with a Little Miss Happiness motif. Wanda looked like Little Miss Total Gloom and Despair, her eyes brimming with tears.

'Please don't be cross with Wanda, Dad. It's all my fault,' I said.

Dad stared at me. Wanda stared at me. I realized they didn't have a clue what I was talking about. They seemed to be discussing something else entirely. It was so weird. Dad was angry and Wanda was upset but I think they were holding hands! They sprang apart the moment they saw me so I can't be sure, but whenever I replay that scene in my head I see their hands, Dad's big pink fingers clasping Wanda's white fists.

Which means . . .

I don't want to think about it. Dad and *Wanda*? He doesn't even like her, I know he doesn't.

He doesn't seem to like me either now. He told me to go upstairs and put some clothes on at once yet there was Wanda in her night things showing heaps more of herself than me. However, I tried very hard indeed not to let it get me down. I am determined not to care about Dad any more. I don't care about Wanda either. They can have as many secrets as they want. I've got *my* secret, my special new friend Treasure.

I told Wanda on the way to school that I was going to come home by myself, just as we'd arranged. She nodded vaguely. It was as if she was plugged into an invisible Walkman, listening to something playing over and over inside her head.

It was not a good day at school. I was last to be

picked for Netball which was totally humiliating. I didn't have anyone to sit with at lunchtime and I'd finished my book (*Zlata's Diary* – but she's not a patch on Anne) so I simply stared into space, pretending I was perfectly content with my own company.

Then in Circle Time we started this discussion about delinquency. Maria and Alice and some of the others were going on and on about yobs on tough estates and how they stole stuff to feed their drug habits and set fire to dustbins and beat up old ladies. I sat there, feeling my face flame as fiery as my hair. Mrs Gibbs said I was uncharacteristically quiet. Did I not have a view on delinquency? So I gave them my view – a panoramic one.

I gave an impassioned speech about Class and Opportunity and the so-called Welfare State (I didn't quite know what I *meant* but it sounded good). Then I talked about the Latimer Estate and how there were lovely, kind, funny, gentle, hospitable people living there, *not* like some posh-nob people who prided themselves on their manners.

There was total silence when I stopped speaking. I found I was panting, as if I'd just run a race. Mrs Gibbs was breathing a little heavily too. 'Well, that's certainly one point of view, India,' she said. 'Does anyone want to take issue with anything India's said?'

No-one said another word! The discussion was over. I'd won – though I knew no-one really agreed with me.

I couldn't wait for school to be finished so I could

rush right round to the Latimer Estate. I shot out of school the moment the bell rang just in case Wanda might be waiting after all. I started to slow down the nearer I got. I was barely putting one foot in front of the other by the time I got to Treasure's block.

I was starting to worry that I'd got it all wrong. It was almost as if I'd made it all up before. I *knew* it wasn't one of my pretend games, I *knew* Treasure was real – but maybe I'd somehow remembered her nicer than she was. Maybe she'd turn out like Maria. Maybe she was secretly laughing at me. Maybe it was all an elaborate game and when I set foot on her territory the boys would barge into me on their skateboards and Treasure would bunny-hop over me on her bike.

I looked all round the play area. I saw the skateboard guys swooping up and down and several kids on bikes – but none of them was Treasure.

I stood still, feeling foolish.

'What are you doing here, Posh Girly?' one the boys yelled.

Another skidded past me, so close I nearly popped the buttons on my school shoes. They all saw and laughed. I tried laughing too, but it just made them sneer more.

'Run away home, Posh Girl, before we give you a good seeing to.'

'I'd like to see you try,' I said, dodging round him, acting as if I couldn't care less though my heart was going *thump thump thump*, like a ball bouncing inside my chest.

'Oi you, where are you off to?' he shouted, as I hurried towards Elm block.

'I'm going to see my friend,' I said.

I didn't want to risk the lift in case they all squeezed in with me. I made for the stairs instead. I ran up. Someone was calling after me, they all started shouting, but I was scared of being ambushed. I went on running up the stairs. Up and up and up. My heart seemed to be a beachball now. I wanted to stop for a rest but I could hear footsteps coming up after me, so I went on running up the stairs. They ran too, getting nearer. Then I tripped rounding the corner of the dark stairwell and sat down hard and they fell over on top of me—

And it was *Treasure*! She'd spotted me when the boys were cheeking me, she'd yelled, they'd yelled, just trying to be helpful.

'I couldn't call properly. I'm so out of breath. Oh help!' She really was wheezing, leaning hard against me as we sat there.

'Shall I fetch your grandma?'

'No, no, I'm fine. Well, I will be in a minute. It's just my asthma. Let me have a little puff.' She fumbled in her schoolbag, found her inhaler and used it. 'There! It was just all that running. I've been charging all the way back from school. I was so worried I'd miss you.'

'I was scared I'd missed *you*. You said you'd be on your bike watching out for me.'

'I know, I know, but I was kept in. That teacher's such a *pig*. They're not supposed to keep you in without proper notice. She said she was just making me tidy up the classroom but everyone had been painting and it took ages.'

'Why was she picking on you? Did you do badly in a test or something?'

I was being sympathetic but Treasure stood up indignantly.

'I was always *top* at my last school. Why do people always think I'm thick? They wanted to stick me in the bottom group here but I wasn't having it.'

'OK, OK. Don't go all ratty, please,' I begged.

'I bet I'm cleverer than you are, even though you're so posh.'

'I'm sure you are,' I said, though actually *I'm* nearly always top, and although I hate my school, it is ultra-academic and competitive. I'm clever but I knew it would be *stupid* to say this to Treasure.

'So what *were* you in trouble for?' I asked.

'I knocked over this girl's paint water kind of acci-dentally on purpose. It splashed her painting so she went wailing to the teacher and then I was for it.'

'But why did you spill her paint water?'

'Because she said stupid things about my nan and my nan's boyfriend and she got on my nerves,' said Treasure, and she spat vehemently down the stairwell.

I very much hoped *I'd* never get on Treasure's nerves.

It was as if she could read my mind. Her hand scrab-bled in around my elbow so we were linked together.

'You're different, India,' she said. She squeezed my

arm tight. 'I was scared you wouldn't come back.'

'I said I would. I promised.'

'I know. But I thought you might have just been messing around, slumming it for a day, seeing how the other half live.'

'I'm not like that.'

'I know you're not.'

'Treasure . . . are we friends?'

'Of course we are.'

'Even though we haven't known each other ages? I used to have this friend Miranda. I've known her since we were babies and we were sort of best friends – but not like *this*. She never even bothered to keep in touch after she left our school.'

'I'll always keep in touch with you,' said Treasure. 'Only I'm not leaving here. I'm staying here for ever and ever and ever. You can be my best friend for ever and ever and ever too.'

Nine

Treasure

Well, the really, truly GREAT thing in my life is that I have a best friend, India. She came calling for me. We went indoors and played with little Britney until Loretta took her round to her friend's flat. Then India and I mucked around with crayons and stickers and glitter, making pictures with Patsy. We didn't really *want* to play with her but we couldn't leave her out.

Patsy drew a little house with three curtained windows and a door with a knocker and a letterbox. She coloured them in very carefully with a bright yellow sun shining above them. She did a strip of blue at the top of her picture for sky and a strip of green grass at the bottom, patterned with a neat row of pink daisies. She stuck a sticker bunny in the grass and a sticker bluebird flying past her sun. She inked MY HOME in silver gel pen at the top and then sat back with a big smile.

'But our home isn't a bit like that,' I said.

'All right,' said Patsy, unfazed. 'It can be the bunny's home.'

'Ah, bless her,' said Nan, throwing chips in the pan with a sizzle.

I made sick noises. Patsy's OK, but I can't stick it when she goes all twee and babyish. Bunny's home, indeed!

'Now, now,' said Nan, putting her hand over my mouth. 'If you're going to be sick go and do it down the toilet, Miss Treasure.' She rested her chin on my head. 'Oh darling,' she said, seeing my picture. Her arms wrapped round me properly.

I'd drawn a dark, horrible home, down at the bottom of my paper, all scribbly black lines, with a tiny woman and some kids like little beetles and a much bigger cartoon ape man going *stamp-stamp-stamp* all over them. Then I'd drawn a ladybird girl in a red fleecy coat flying up, up, up to a new brightly coloured home at the top of a multi-storey block of flats. I'd emptied practically the whole of Patsy's glitter on the fourth flat of the fourteenth floor.

'That's lovely, Treasure,' said Nan, giving me another hug.

Then she had a peer at India's picture. She'd drawn a very tall thin house that took up the whole of her paper.

'You live in a big house, darling,' said Nan, trying to act like she wasn't dead impressed.

I peered at it too, wondering why she'd drawn some kind of sinister army marching along outside. There was a river too, though we're nowhere near the Thames.

'It's not *my* home,' said India. 'It's Anne Frank's house.'

'Who's Anne, sweetheart?' said Nan.

India looked astonished. 'Don't you know who *Anne Frank* is?' she said.

She didn't mean to be rude but it came out that way. Her posh little voice didn't help.

'Sorry, dear, I don't,' said Nan, going pink. She didn't sound sorry, she sounded dead snippy.

My tummy went tight. I couldn't stand it if Nan took against India. But it was OK. India had gone pink too. She said quickly and humbly, 'Oh, I'm ever so sorry, Mrs Mitchell.'

'Rita,' said Nan, nice again.

'It's just that Anne Frank is my all-time heroine. She was this Jewish girl who hid from the Nazis in Holland during the war—'

And then I got it – the long thin Dutch house and the canal and the scary soldiers. I peered more closely at India's picture and saw the top of the house was turned into a hidey hole. You could just see Anne through the window, writing in a little red notebook.

'Her diary,' said India reverently.

'I keep a diary,' I said, and then I blushed in case it

sounded stupid. I hope Willie didn't hear. I'd hate it if he leafed through this and had a right laugh at me. Patsy was too busy shaking glitter over her picture to take in what I was saying. Her bunny was rapidly turning into Rhinestone Rabbit.

'I keep a diary too!' said India, and then *she* blushed.

'You girls!' said Nan. 'Well, I *don't* keep a diary. I'm not confiding my secrets to anyone!'

India went on telling us about Anne Frank for *ages*, until to be honest we were all a little bit sick of her. It got more interesting when India started going on about Anne and her parents and this boy Peter who hid in the secret annexe with them. Anne falls in love with him at the end of the book and he's her boyfriend. India sighed heavily when she said this.

'He doesn't seem *worthy* of her,' she said. 'Still, it wasn't as if she really had any choice stuck in the annexe.'

'Yes she did. She could choose not to have a boyfriend at all,' I said.

'Do you have a boyfriend, Treasure?'

'No way! I can't *stick* boys.'

Well, Willie's OK, I suppose. He does let me borrow his bike. And he lets me wear his Tommy Hilfiger sweatshirt. It's not even an old one, it's one he often wears himself, but when I said I thought it looked great he just took it off and shoved it over my head.

'Looks great on you too, little Treas,' he said.

It looks literally great, way down to my knees, but I kind of like the baggy look. I kind of like Willie too.

But that's OK because he's family. I'm never ever going to get a *boyfriend*.

My mum would be great if it wasn't for her *blankety blankety blank* boyfriends. Especially Terry.

I'm so scared. It's Saturday tomorrow. Mum phoned up again last night to say they really *are* coming to get me.

Nan took the phone and told Mum she was talking rubbish.

'No I am not,' said Mum. 'I've consulted a solicitor, see. He says there's no question, Treasure's mine and she belongs here with me.'

'But that animal you live with whipped her with his belt,' Nan exploded.

'No he never. And anyway, even if he did, which he *didn't*, you've no proof. Now listen, if you don't hand Treasure over when we come for her we're getting a court order.'

'You can get the Queen herself to command me. I don't give a stuff,' said Nan, tucking me tight under her arm. 'No-one's taking my Treasure away. Let's just ask *her* what she wants.'

'It's what the courts say. We've got a foolproof case. I'm her *mother*,' said Mum.

'And I'm *your* mother, God help me, and I just want to do what's best for your child,' said Nan.

'Now look, Rita—' It was Terry suddenly speaking. I shrunk back, pressing my head into Nan's soft chest so I couldn't hear him.

I just heard the buzz of his voice. He wasn't

shouting. He didn't sound drunk. He was using his wheedling *I'm-a-really-nice-guy* tone. But he's often like that just before he pounces. Nan wasn't fooled. Her nose wrinkled like there was a terrible smell as he whined and whinged into her ear.

'I *am* being reasonable, Terry,' she said. 'You're the guy who can't keep his belt buckled.'

Terry's voice buzzed louder, like he was threatening her. Nan stood firm. But she started to shiver, even though the heating's always turned full up in the flat.

'What? What's he saying? Nan, what *is* it?'

She patted me on the shoulder to keep me quiet. Then she drew in her breath sharply.

'It wasn't *murder*. Even the cops knew that. It was an accident. Don't you dare talk about my Pete like that,' she said, and she slammed the phone down.

I waited. I was shivering too. Nan held me tight but she didn't speak. When I looked up there were tears glistening on the end of her eyelashes.

'Oh Nan!'

'Now it's OK, Treasure. I'm getting in a silly tizz over nothing. Don't take any notice of silly old Nan.'

'You promise promise promise I can still stay with you?'

'I promise promise promise,' she said – but she didn't look me in the eyes.

I caught her by the cheeks and tilted her head.

'Nan! Look, I'm not a little kid.'

'You're the littlest kid ever,' said Nan. 'Barely bigger than Britney.' Tears were spilling down her cheeks now.

99

'Did Terry say he'd get *you*, Nan?'

'It's not that, pet. I'd like to see him try. No, it's just something he said about you living here with my Pete . . .'

I didn't understand. 'But he's . . . not here,' I said delicately.

'Yes, I know, pet, but he's only got another six months to go if he gets his good behaviour taken into consideration, and Pete's no fool, he's sweet as pie to everyone so he can get right back to his family as soon as possible. That's what that wicked Terry is on about. He says these social worker busybodies won't let you stay with me, not with a guy who's got a lot of previous, and a five stretch for manslaughter. He was even saying they'll think about taking Patsy into care, but that's ludicrous, he's her *father*.'

'Well, he's my grandfather.'

'Not really, Treasure. Not by blood.'

I suddenly feel like I've been left one side of a mountain range and Nan and Pete and Loretta and baby Britney and Willie and Patsy are all on the other side. There's no way I can leap over to be with them. I'm stuck all by myself . . . and Terry's climbing up after me, my side of the mountain.

'We'll tell on him. We'll show my scar,' I said.

'Yes, we can try, my love, but remember what we said up the hospital, that you got hurt after a game with your brother and sister? It would be hard to go back on that in court.'

'So do you think they'll really take us to court, Nan?'

'No, darling, I'm sure Terry's just trying to scare us,' said Nan. 'All this solicitor talk! I bet they're bluffing.'

'So are they still coming tomorrow or is that a bluff too?' I asked, trying to stop my voice going squeaky.

'I'm not sure, sweetheart,' said Nan. 'But never you mind. You don't even have to be here. I'm not having you traumatized by that pig all over again. Yes, that's it, my pet, you can have a day out. Maybe up to town, eh? You leave it to Nan. Don't look so tragic. You're not to worry.'

I can't help it. It feels like I've swallowed a whole hive of bees and they're all buzzing inside my stomach.

I can't sleep.

I'm scared of sleeping, because every time I start dreaming Terry jumps out at me and he's whirling that belt, going *crack crack crack* with it like a whip. I wake with such a start and each time I tell myself it's OK, it's just a bad dream, but then I remember Terry isn't a dream, he's real, and he's coming to get me. He's acting all soft and sweet like he really loves me and wants me back but I know just what will happen once he gets me behind closed doors.

Ten

India

Dear Kitty

I woke up early this morning and sat cross-legged on my bed writing my diary. Every time I wrote my friend's name, Treasure, I spread it out in very careful twirly, fancy lettering and highlighted it in gold until page after page glowed. Then I realized I was starving so I padded downstairs to fix myself some breakfast.

I'd just made myself a most interesting jumbo sandwich – a layer of banana, cream cheese and honey and then another contrasting layer of chocolate spread and peach slices – when Mum came bursting into the kitchen, startling me so that I dropped a bottle of milk all over the floor.

'For goodness sake, India, do you have to be so

102

clumsy?' she said, leaping about with paper towels and kitchen cloths. 'And what exactly are you eating?'

'Just a sandwich.'

'It looks more like an entire loaf of bread to me,' said Mum, mopping. 'You don't seem to be taking your diet very seriously, India.'

She pointedly put two lemons into the blender. *Mum's* breakfast.

She always goes on and on and on about my diet as if my size is the only significant thing about me. The blender rattled away. Mum looked at me. Maybe she was wondering if she could stuff me in along with the lemons and squeeze me right down to the pulp. I doubt I'd fit into a Moya Upton outfit even then.

I took a large defiant bite of my sandwich, smacking my lips. Mum sighed and switched off the blender. She poured her juice and drank it up. Her cheeks sucked in a little at the sourness but she'd rather die than add a little sugar.

'I think you're anorexic, Mum,' I said.

'Don't be ridiculous. I just care about my body. It's time you took a little care of yourself too, India, now you're growing up.'

She said the words *growing up* with extreme emphasis, as if I was shooting straight up to the ceiling and spreading till I could touch all the walls at once. Roll up, roll up, to see the Incredible Growing Girl, twenty metres high, 1000 kilos and rapidly increasing. It's pretty humiliating when your own mother treats you like a circus freak.

'You'll turn *me* anorexic if you carry on nagging me about my weight,' I said, bolting the last of my sandwich.

Mum gave this horrible false tinkly laugh. 'That'll be the day!'

She said it spitefully, as sour as her lemon juice. I turned my back on her, opening the fridge up, pretending to be searching for more food. I didn't want her to see the tears in my eyes.

'India?'

'*What?*' I said, as rudely as I dared, my head still in the fridge. I wondered if my tears would turn into tiny stalactites if I stayed there long enough.

'I'm sorry, sweetie. I didn't mean to hurt your feelings,' she said softly. Well, as soft as she gets.

She didn't mean to hurt my feelings? She expects it to feel like fun when your own mother implies you are GROSS?

I felt like I was growing a frosty mask inside the fridge. She was sorry for me now. Well, I *could* tell her straight, 'Don't feel sorry for me, Mum, feel sorry for yourself. Everyone hates you. Even Dad prefers Wanda to you.'

I wouldn't say it. But thinking it made me feel better. I straightened up and smiled calmly at my mother.

'I'm fine, Mum, really.'

'What are your plans for today, darling?' she said, sitting on a kitchen stool and crossing one long, elegant, tanned hairless leg over the other. She wears

104

matching silk nighties and negligées in subtle strange colours, inky-blue with pink lace, forest green with turquoise lace, coffee with tangerine lace. I used to love her nighties. I liked sneaking into Mum's bedroom and dressing up in their silky softness, playing at being a princess.

I couldn't stick wearing anything of Mum's now. Well. They wouldn't fit anyway.

Mum always wants me to have *plans*. She can't ever let me drift through the day doing just what I feel like. She has the engagement diary approach to life. She'd like every half hour of my day filled in.

I shrugged and mumbled something about homework.

'Oh darling, you and your homework!' she said, as if it's my personal eccentricity.

She is the only mother in my class who really doesn't care about her daughter's marks. She seems to find it vaguely embarrassing when I come top.

'And I'm going to read this new book about Anne Frank.'

'I know Anne Frank's story is very moving, India, but don't you think it's a little morbid being *so* obsessed by her?'

'No, I think it's perfectly normal. She's my hero, my inspiration.'

Mum gave a little snort. She was laughing at me. I tried to think of the frost in the fridge but I couldn't stop my face turning beetroot red.

'Well, I'm going to get into my running things,' said

Mum, swallowing the last of her lemon. She put her head on one side. 'I don't suppose you'd care to join me?'

I bared my teeth in a grin to make it plain I knew she was joking.

'Maybe we can go shopping together when I get back?' said Mum.

I think she must have read some article about high-powered career mums spending 'quality time' with their daughters. But I hate, hate, hate shopping with Mum. I like *shopping*, so long as it's *my* way. Wanda and I go to Woolworths or Wilkinsons, where everything is bright and cheap, and we play this game seeing how many things we can buy for a fiver. I like choosing girly notebooks with pink checks and puppies and gel pens and peachy sweet scent and little floppy toy animals and lots and lots and lots of pick-'n'mix sweets. Then we go to McDonald's and I have a McFlurry and if it goes down too quickly I'll have another. And maybe even another if Wanda is in a truly good mood. Sadly she hasn't been in a good mood for ages.

I wonder if I should try talking to her? Try to comfort her, maybe – because this thing with Dad seems to be making her so unhappy.

It makes *me* feel unhappy thinking about her and Dad. If I didn't love him I think maybe I'd hate him – the way I hate Mum.

I don't really hate her.

Yes I do.

I *certainly* hate her when we go shopping together. We nearly always have to go to the places that stock Moya Upton clothes. She has a sneaky check on the stock. The salesgirls generally twig who she is and go into a twitter. There's often a rich mother with some horrible, pretty, skinny daughter trying on the latest little Moya Upton number and they go all squeaky when they're introduced to Mum. Sometimes they get her to do the dumbest stuff like sign her own label. All the time they're admiring Mum their eyes keep swivelling round to me as if they can't believe that I can possibly be her *daughter*.

I sometimes long to be an orphan.

Mum came back into the kitchen in her tiny grey jogging suit. She waggled her manicured nails at me and then darted off out the back door. She looked like a sleek slim rat, whiskers well shaved, eyes bright and beady. This does not sound flattering, I know. But if *I* were squeezed into her grey jogging suit another obvious animal springs – no, *lumbers* – into my mind's eye. It is gross to compare your mother to a rodent. It is even grosser to know that she thinks of you as an elephant. Not just your mother. Lots and lots and lots of people make pachyderm remarks when I'm around.

Maybe it's not so bad. Elephants are intelligent animals. They are meant to have superb memories. It sounds like boasting, but my own memory is phenomenal. I can quote long passages of Anne's diary by heart now.

I shall lend it to Treasure because I just know she'll

love it too. I re-read a few favourite parts while I ate another little breakfast. (I'd discovered Wanda's pop-tarts tucked at the back of the larder. She seems to have lost her appetite recently but mine is ever-present.) Then I wrote more of my own diary. Wanda was up by this time, yawning and sighing.

'What's *up*, Wanda?'

She looked at me, shrugged and flicked her long wet hair out of her face, making a tiny rainstorm over her shoulders.

'Is it Dad?'

She jumped as if I'd shot at her. 'No! What do you mean? Are those *my* pop-tarts you're eating? Stop it, you greedy girl! Your dad! Why should I be upset about your dad?'

It's *definitely* my dad.

She drifted off, saying she was going to dry her hair. I heard her going *mutter-mutter* upstairs with Dad.

Then five minutes later Dad bounded into the kitchen, all wired up. Clicking his fingers and tutting his tongue against his teeth. He came out with all this guff about poor Wanda being homesick. Do they think I'm mad? I know what's going on. I think *they're* mad. Dad liked Wanda's friend Suzi a lot more than Wanda herself. Everyone could see that at the New Year's Eve party – even Wanda. And what is she doing getting mixed up with my dad? He's old enough to be *her* dad too.

I don't understand love affairs. I'm not ever going to make a fool of myself that way. I'm *sooooo* glad

Treasure hasn't got a boyfriend. I don't want one either.

I hope we'll stay friends until we're grown up and then we could maybe share a flat together. I wonder what Treasure wants to be when she grows up? I want to be a writer, of course, just like Anne. It would be great if my books became big, big hits so that I don't have to use a penny of Mum and Dad's money. Yes, I shall earn all my own money – heaps of it – and then even if Treasure doesn't have a well-paid job it won't matter a bit because I could take care of the rent.

If my books don't sell well it won't really matter. We could make do with a very modest flat. We could maybe even rent one on the Latimer Estate. Then Treasure's family could come and visit every day. I don't think I want my family to visit at all. Not even Dad. He hates the Latimer Estate.

We drove through it after lunch. I was feeling sick. Dad said he'd take me out to lunch, just us two, anywhere I wanted. I was thrilled he was in a good mood for once. I thought hard, trying to think of the perfect place. I thought Dad would like somewhere really fancy and sophisticated. I remembered this lovely Italian place we went to once on Mum's birthday.

'Let's go to La Terrazza!' I said.

'Oh for God's sake, India,' Dad shouted.

It was the worst choice ever. I hadn't realized it was terribly expensive. Dad went on and on about it, asking if I thought he was made of money. He thought

I'd choose McDonald's like any other kid, maybe Pizza Express if I was pushing it – but La Terrazza was ridiculous. Still, he'd said I could go anywhere, so fine, right, never let it be said that he couldn't keep his word. I was practically in tears by this time. I told him that I didn't really want to go to La Terrazza and I'd *love* to go to McDonald's – but Dad wouldn't drop it. He took me to La Terrazza and I chose the dish of the day because it was supposed to be a bargain. It was a seafood spaghetti dish that looked horribly like cooked worms and slugs. I pretended it was delicious. I said I was having a lovely time. I told Dad he was wonderful, giving me such a treat. Dad ate lots too – and he drank a bottle of wine.

I thought we'd leave the car outside the restaurant and get a taxi back home but Dad opened the car door, gesturing for me to get inside. I didn't know what to do. I knew he shouldn't be driving after all that drink (he'd also had a brandy while I struggled with three scoops of ice-cream) but I didn't dare say anything in case he got mad again. He'd cheered up now. He said I was his little princess, the number-one girl in his life.

So the number-one girl got in the car and crossed her fingers and prayed. He drove carefully enough, singing cod-Pavarotti arias: 'Oh, La Terrazza, all the waiters are Prats-sa, we'll give them no tips, why can't we eat ch-i-ps . . .' I laughed as if I thought he was the funniest man ever, peering out of the window as we drove through the Latimer Estate. I looked out for

Treasure. I wanted to tell Dad all about her but I knew it wouldn't work.

One of the skateboarding boys swooped danger-ously close to our car, only just jumping off in time, his skateboard going clunk against our bumper. Dad braked furiously and leapt out the car. He shouted at the boy. The boy shouted something much ruder back, and stuck his finger up in the air before running away. While Dad was angrily examining his scratched paint-work, Mrs Watkins who lives next door to Treasure's nan came shuffling past, her weird grown-up son loping along beside her, swinging their Safeway's bags.

'Watch them bags, Michael! Don't bash them like that,' she grumbled.

'Sorry, Mum,' Michael said meekly – but when he saw me sitting in the car he stuck his tongue out and waggled it behind his mother's back. I smiled politely. Dad looked up, frowning at both of us. He got back in the car, slamming the door.

'What a stinky dumping ground this is,' he said, driving away. 'Foul-mouthed little vandals and total nutters. They should all be locked up. I wish we didn't live so close by.'

I wondered what Dad would say if he knew I'd been to tea here with my best friend. I was desperate to see her again but I knew it was better to bide my time. When we got back home Wanda greeted us wistfully, asking all about the meal. I felt bad, wishing Dad had invited her too. Mum was out again. She'd left a note

111

to say she'd gone to an art exhibition with Bella, Miranda's mum.

'Big Belly-Button,' said Dad, crumpling up the note.

Bella isn't really big, she's got a lovely figure, and her belly is as flat as a pancake but Dad always acts like she looks awful. Maybe he tried to chat her up once and she wasn't interested? I quite like chatting to Bella myself because she treats me like a real person and she doesn't always seem to be sniggering up her sleeve at me. I'd have normally been hurt that they hadn't asked me along too. I'd been wanting to find out how Miranda is getting on at boarding school – but now I couldn't give two hoots. I'm not bothered about boring old Miranda any more. I don't think she ever really wanted to be my friend. Anyway, I've got a much, much, much better friend now. And with Mum out of the way maybe I could sneak out to see her.

Dad said he had to catch up with some figurework and went off to his study. Wanda trailed along after him, wondering if she could help. Wanda, who can't even count her change properly! Dad screwed up his face and sighed at her, so she sloped off, looking mournful. I don't know what she *sees* in him.

I waited half an hour, racing through my weekend homework to while away the time. I heard clinking and little *glug-glug-glug* sounds from Dad's study. He was having even more to drink. He'd be seeing double when he looked at those figures.

I hovered in the hall. I heard Wanda in the living

room whispering on the phone. I hoped she was talking to all her relatives in Australia. Serve Dad right if he had to pay a massive bill. I walked heavily up the stairs to my room in case Dad or Wanda were listening – and then tiptoed down a minute later, *sooo* softly, right along the hall and out the front door. I shut it behind me very slowly so that it clicked shut with scarcely a sound.

I stood outside in my own driveway, took a deep breath, and then set out for the Latimer Estate. Treasure would be so surprised. I'd thought I'd only be able to see her after school but now there seemed no reason at all why I couldn't slip away at the weekend too whenever I had the chance.

Treasure wasn't in the grounds on her bike. I asked one of the skateboarding boys if he'd seen Treasure but he just shrugged. At least he didn't call names after me. I looked more normal in my Saturday jeans and sweatshirt and jacket (all from Gap – absolutely *not* Moya Upton). I was dying to show Treasure I don't always look like I've stepped straight out of *The Twins at St Clare's*.

I opted for the stair route so I was breathless by the time I got to Treasure's landing. I hurried past Mrs Watkins and Mumbly Michael's flat and knocked on Treasure's door. Her grandma answered it. She looked different, older somehow, and her hair was all tousled as if she'd been running her fingers through it.

'Oh, it's you . . . India,' she said, obviously barely remembering my name.

'Can I see Treasure?'

She swallowed, glancing behind her. 'She's not here, pet. She's gone out with the other kids.'

'Oh. Well, do you know when she'll be back?'

She looked anxious and shook her head. Someone was shouting inside her flat. Some man.

'You'd better run back home, dear,' Nan said.

This man suddenly came out into the hall, a horrible man in a check shirt and black jeans, his dirty-blond hair all greasy and flopping over his forehead. His eyes were green and glacial.

'Who are you?' he said, glaring at me.

I knew who *he* was. Terry, Treasure's stepfather. The one who marked her face. I looked at his waist. There was the belt. I saw the buckle and shivered.

'It's just a little girl from up Parkfield,' said Nan. She nodded at me. 'Off you go, pet.'

But the Belt Man stepped forward. 'Are you a pal of Treasure's, eh?'

I nodded.

'So where is she, then?'

'I don't know.'

'Of course she doesn't know, Terry. She thought she was *here*.'

'Or maybe Treasure sent her, to see if me and her mum had cleared off yet?' said Terry. He suddenly seized me by the shoulders.

'Leave that kid *alone*, Terry,' said Nan sharply.

He loosened his grip a little. 'You're *sure* you don't know where Treasure is?'

114

I shook my head, trying to act like he couldn't scare me.

'Let her *go*,' said Nan.

'I'm not doing anything to her,' said Terry. He put his head close to mine. 'Well, listen here, sweetheart. You tell your little pal Treasure she's to stop playing us up and come on home. She's making her mum poorly. You tell her, right?'

'I'll tell her if I see her,' I said, wriggling my shoulders free.

'That's it, lovie, you scoot off home,' said Nan.

I ran all the way. I forgot to be cautious going back. Dad heard the front door and came out into the hall.

'India?' He blinked at me, looking fuddled. 'Have you been out?'

'Yes, but just . . . just to the shop on the corner.'

Dad's face cleared. 'Ah! Chocolate?'

'Don't tell Mum when she comes back, will you?'

He grinned and put his fingers to his lips. 'Your secret's safe with me.'

He slurred the *s*'s a bit but I pretended not to notice he was drunk. Dad frightens me sometimes now because he's so moody – but he's nowhere *near* as scary as Terry.

Poor, poor Treasure. I'm so scared for her.

Eleven

Treasure

I don't know what to do. I've been sitting in McDonald's for hours and hours. We've had a Big Mac and French fries, then Cokes, then ice-cream with butterscotch sauce, then more Cokes, and then one further portion of French fries between us. Willie's gone to have another scout round to see if Terry's van is still parked at our flats. He'll ring if it's safe to come back. I've got Loretta's mobile. She's gone home with Britney. It's OK, Terry won't pick on her. It's only me he's after.

Patsy should go back too. She's curled up in the corner with my new red coat over her as a blanket. It arrived this morning. I love it. I hope Patsy doesn't dribble on it. She's sucking her thumb, nearly asleep.

She's been crying. Terry wouldn't go for her – Nan would tear his head off his shoulders if he did – but she might panic and blurt out where I am. Loretta's too canny to give so much as a hint and Britney can't talk so I don't have to worry about them.

It's been such a *long* day. It was fun at first. Nan gave us each five whole pounds and we went round the market for ages choosing stuff. I bought a new big, fat spiral notebook with a gold cover because I've filled up every single page of the Terry Torture book with my diary entries. Patsy bought a little pink glittery notebook and some pink daisy hairslides. Willie bought a weird garage CD and two old copies of *Viz* off a second-hand stall. Loretta donated her fiver to Britney and bought her three yellow plastic ducks with orange beaks, the sort you float in the bath. Britney always grizzles and fusses when Loretta baths her, though she's fine when I have a go, splashing round like a little water-baby, but it would NOT be tactful to point this out. As soon as she spotted the ducks Britney loved them and wanted them right now, this instant. She didn't want to hold just one, she wanted to clutch all three, which is a bit of a job if you've got normal-size hands and totally impossible if you're a baby. After a great deal of fussing we got her holding the big mother duck with the two duck-lings tucked either side of Britney in her buggy.

Britney was so excited she kept trying to kiss the big duck and getting pecked all over with its plastic beak. She had little pink peck marks on her cheeks and

117

forehead but she didn't seem to mind a bit. I said, 'Yes, Britney, duck! Lovely duck, three lovely ducks. Who's a lucky girl to have a duck, eh?' so often that she seemed to get the hang of talking too and said 'duck' herself, over and over. Only she hasn't got enough teeth to make a clear 'd' sound so it seemed like she was swearing and we all burst out laughing.

Then we took her to the park and we all had a swing. I started showing off, climbing up the rusty swing poles and hanging by my hands from the top. Patsy squealed and Loretta nagged but Willie was dead impressed, I could tell. He tried to shin up himself but he kept slipping down. He said it was because his hands were sweaty, but that was an excuse. Then a green mini-van pulled up and I started sweating myself but it wasn't Terry, it was just a woman with a whole load of dogs, though it made me start worrying all the same. I thought we shouldn't be hanging around somewhere like the park. It was one of the first places Terry might come looking for me.

I couldn't think where else we could go. Patsy was starting to droop a bit and Britney was getting hungry and needed changing.

'We'll go round my friend Marianne's,' said Loretta.

'What, all of us?' said Willie, pulling a face. 'I can't stick your mate Marianne.'

'You don't have to come too, Willie,' I said. 'You can go off with your mates if you want.'

Willie thought about it. Then he shook his head.

'Nah, it's OK. I'll come with you lot. If Terry tracks

you down you'll need me to protect you, right?'

I threw my arms round him I was so touched. Willie went red and wriggled away as soon as possible. I thanked him. I thanked them all.

'Put a sock in it, Treasure,' said Loretta. 'Don't go on like that in front of Marianne or I'll be dead embarrassed.'

Loretta got to know Marianne when she was in hospital having Britney. Marianne had a little boy on the same day, called Tim, only she calls him Tigger and dresses him in these cute little orange-and-black stripey outfits. Tigger certainly roars like a tiger. When he and Britney are both having a cry you can't hear yourself think. But that was great, because I didn't *want* to think, not about Terry and Mum round at Nan's.

I wasn't all that keen on Marianne either. She's nineteen and yet she acts like she's Patsy's age. It's daft, the council have given her this smashing flat and yet she can't get her act together and keep it clean. She can't do the simplest things like turn on the boiler or get the phone connected. The council won't give Loretta her own place because she's only fifteen but she's heaps more sensible than Marianne. Loretta wants to move in with her which seems a great idea, but her social worker thinks this mightn't be a good idea. She thinks they might go out clubbing and leave the babies on their own.

'Cheek!' said Loretta, heating up a bottle for Britney in Marianne's cold and grubby kitchen. 'As if we would!'

'Well, I'd always babysit for you if you *did* fancy a night out,' I offered.

'That's sweet of you, Treasure. You're great with Britney, I know.' Loretta paused. 'Maybe that's why your mum's desperate to get you back. Do you help her out a lot with baby Gary?'

'Yeah, but he's nowhere near as cute as Britney. Anyway, she'll have to manage. I'm not *going* back.'

'Of course you're not,' said Loretta. 'Not with that Terry around. I don't know what's up with your mum. If any bloke of mine hit Britney he'd be out on his ear. Not that I'm that fussed about blokes if Britney's dad is a shining example. Nah, soon as I'm sixteen, seventeen tops, I'll nag for my own flat just like this one. Then you could always come and live with Britney and me, Treasure.'

'No, Treasure and *me* are going to share a flat the minute we leave school,' said Patsy, doing a little grapevine-chassez-kick-ball-change routine up and down the tiled floor.

'Well, *I'm* not sharing a flat with Treasure,' said Willie, grinning. 'It would cramp my style with all my girlfriends!'

But Willie stayed with me at Marianne's all afternoon, sprawling in one of her slippery leatherette armchairs, yawning and cracking his knuckles and sighing, not even able to watch television because Marianne's set has gone on the blink and she hasn't done anything about getting it fixed. We used the babies like little television sets, all of us sitting gawping at them as they lay on their backs and kicked on Marianne's dusty hearthrug. It's black-and-orange striped acrylic so Tigger in his tiger playsuit blended in so completely Patsy didn't notice he was there and very nearly trod on him.

Loretta phoned Nan at four but it was obvious my Mum and Terry were still grimly sitting it out with Bethany and Kyle and little Gary. She heard him grizzling in the background.

So we sat on too, waiting and waiting, until Britney started to fuss for another feed. Loretta didn't have any more bottles. Marianne didn't have the right formula as she's put Tigger on cow's milk already, so Loretta had to take Britney home.

Willie and Patsy and I stayed on at Marianne's for a bit but then her new boyfriend came round on his way home from work and it was obvious we were in the way. So we cleared off. Patsy and I are hanging out at McDonald's now, like I said, and Willie's just rung and Terry's van is *still* there.

I don't know what to do. They're obviously camping out at Nan's all day. Maybe all night too. I don't know what to do or where to go.

Patsy's woken up again now but she's a bit sniffly. Two different mums have clucked over her and asked me if we're all right. I keep saying yes, we're fine, but we're not. We can't stay here much longer.

A *third* woman has just come up and asked where our mother is. We both said, truthfully, that she's at home. Then this woman shook her head at us and said that *we* should be at home too, and didn't we have anyone looking after us? I told her, equally truthfully, that my uncle was going to meet up with us soon. That reassured her a little, but she did shake her head again over Patsy.

I'm worried about her. She's trying to be so good. Every so often she reaches up and puts her arm round me and tells *me* not to worry – but she keeps on crying. I've used up half the paper napkins in McDonald's mopping her.

Later. Much, much later! You will never, ever, ever guess where I am!

OK, I was in McDonald's with Patsy and then the mobile rings again, and *this* time Willie's all excited. He was walking back into town when he saw Terry in the van driving off.

'You're *sure* it was him? There are heaps of vans like his,' I said.

Willie said he'd seen Terry at the wheel, my mum beside him with the baby on her lap. It was definitely them. They'd really and truly gone.

I gave Patsy a big hug and told her we could go home at long last. She burst into a fresh flood of tears because she was so happy. We set off hand in hand. Patsy was so relieved to be going home at last she perked up and skipped and sashayed all the way down the road. I did too, even though my last year's boots were pinching and there was still a flicker of fear in my stomach.

Willie was waiting for us at the end of Latimer Road, jumping up and down on someone's little garden wall like he was doing step exercises. When he saw us coming he waved in mid-step, slipped and landed on his knees. It must have hurt horribly and we heard some pretty impressive swearing, but when we reached him he was all smiles.

'He's gone, he's gone! And if he comes back I'll sort him out, don't you worry, Treasure,' Willie said, squaring his shoulders.

We both knew Terry could knock Willie flying using just his little finger but I grinned at him gratefully. The three of us set off through the estate. Patsy did her little dance and Willie borrowed a skateboard and did a few super-nifty swirls and swoops in celebration. I had a go too. I didn't quite get the knack at first and kept tipping it up. Willie enjoyed crowing that I was useless – but then he showed me how to place my feet and the right way to lean and I was suddenly off, swooping along, gathering speed, my new glasses slipping, my hair streaming, my mouth screaming . . .

I heard this car behind me and I thought, Oh help, how do I stop? Still, all the cars slow down for skateboarders, even though the drivers shout and swear a bit. But this car seemed to be revving up so I swerved to one side, trying to look round. I swerved too far and fell right off.

It wasn't a car. It was a van. A green van. It was Terry back. He'd played a trick on us. He hadn't really gone. He'd waited for Willie to give me the tip off and now he'd ambushed us.

I saw Mum. She was out of the van first, almost dropping baby Gary, clutching him to her hip with one hand.

'*Treasure!*' she cried. It sounded like she really cared. My heart turned over. Maybe I'd been an idiot. What was I doing, running away from my own mum? I loved her. I loved her just as much as Nan. She needed me—

But then Terry jumped out the other side of the van. He was smiling. It wasn't a *pleased to see you, we've really missed you, sorry about hitting you with my belt, I'll never touch you again, I swear* smile.

Oh no. It was the look a cat gets when it pounces on a fledgling. His eyes were gleaming but they were like slithers of green glass.

'Well, well, well, it's Treasure!' he said. 'You've led us a merry dance today, sweetheart. Still, we've got you now.'

They'll never ever get me. I was up and off, on the skateboard, one mad thrust of my left foot and then I was careering past him, past Mum, past Bethany and Kyle peering boggle-eyed from the van, while Willie and Patsy and the kid who owned the skateboard all yelled after me.

I swooped along wildly towards Nan's block. I heard Terry and Mum piling back into the van, slamming the doors, starting up the engine ready to come after me. I aimed the skateboard towards the steps where the van couldn't follow me.

Mumbly Michael was throwing bundles of rubbish away in the dark dustbin recess. He stopped, his glasses glinting as he saw me flying along, Terry in the van after me, Willie and Patsy shouting their heads off. I slid off the skateboard and made it to the steps. I started to run up – but this hand shot out in the dark and grabbed my wrist.

I gasped and tugged but the hand hung on. It was Michael mumbling something at me. I thought he was saying 'hi' over and over – but then I got it. He was saying 'hide'. So I stayed there in the dark with him, hiding in the smelly dustbin recess. I heard Terry go leaping up the stairs two at a time towards Nan's, everyone following him.

I clung onto Michael. He held me quietly, gently patting my back with the pads of his fingers. We stood silently while the footsteps grew fainter – and then far away I heard hammering on Nan's door and shouting, lots of shouting, Terry, Mum, Willie, then Nan. Another door banged and Mrs Watkins joined in too.

'Mum!' said Michael. 'My mum, nag nag nag.' He paused. 'That man chasing you. Is he your dad?'

'No! He's just my mum's bloke. I hate him. He's trying to get me back. Oh, Michael, what am I going to do? He'll be after me again in a minute.'

'Run for it,' said Michael. 'I wish I could run for it. Run from my mum.'

I'd thought he loved his mum. Maybe he only

stayed because he didn't have any place else to go.

'You come too,' I said.

I was so scared I needed someone, anyone, even Michael. He clasped my hand and went out the dustbin recess, blinking in the sudden bright light. We ran round the edge of the courtyard, keeping close to the wall so Terry couldn't look down from the balcony and spot us. We got all the way round to the end of our Elm block and on up to Sycamore and Beech.

'What are you up to, Michael?' one woman said, as we dodged past her. 'Hey, come back! What will your mum say?'

'Don't care,' Michael panted. He was slowing down now, gasping for breath, his big face bright red and sweating.

He leant against the wall, shutting his eyes.

'Come on, Michael, quick! He'll come after us!'

Michael's chest was heaving up and down.

'I . . . can't.'

'You *can*. Run!'

'You run. I'm . . .' He gestured to show he didn't have the breath – or the bottle.

I couldn't waste any more time persuading him.

'OK. Thanks then. Bye.'

I was much quicker without him, off in a flash, round every corner, out of the estate in a jiffy, veering down side roads to throw Terry off the trail. I was running like crazy but I didn't know where I was going. I couldn't run for ever. I didn't have any money left. I couldn't even go back to McDonald's.

I went back to Marianne's, making up a whole deal in my head, ready to offer her a total babycare service, plus all the cooking and cleaning, if she'd just let me kip on her sofa for a bit. But she didn't answer her door even though I banged and banged. I knew she was in there, with her boyfriend. I tried begging her through the letterbox but she took no notice.

I gave up and trailed off, my toes stubbed at every step in my tight boots. My tummy felt like it was tipping right over. I had to nip down an alleyway to be sick. I tried hard to do it neatly but I couldn't help some of it splashing on my lovely new red coat. I nearly cried then.

I wondered whether to give up and go back to Nan's. Maybe it wouldn't be so bad back at my old home. Maybe if I learnt to button my lip Terry wouldn't go for me so much. Maybe I could make myself so useful with the kids and the housework Mum would start loving me at last. Maybe Kyle would stop kicking me and Bethany and I would be best friends.

I knew it was all rubbish. And if I went back they'd never let me stay at Nan's again.

I'd never see India either.

India.

I thought hard, mopping at my coat with a little wad of tissue. I stood on one foot and then the other to ease the pain of my sore toes. I argued it out in my head.

I could go to India.

No, I couldn't. She lived in *Parkfield*.

So? I could go and visit her. She'd been round to visit me.

Yes, but that was different. I couldn't just turn up on her doorstep. I didn't even know which house she lived in.

I could find out.

I couldn't go round like this, all scruffy and stained. Her mum would have a fit. She was posh. She'd treat me like dirt.

India wouldn't. She was my friend.

I went on saying it over and over as I limped along towards Parkfield. I didn't know which *bit* of Parkfield to aim at. It was bigger than I'd thought, street after street of these huge posh houses, but they weren't called *streets*, they were avenues and drives and closes. It all seemed so empty. There are always kids playing out on the Latimer Estate and old ladies having a moan and old men having a curse and a spit and lads larking and girls giggling and there are dogs all over even though the council says you're not allowed pets.

I couldn't see a single kid playing out in Parkfield, not even skipping in their lovely landscaped gardens. Perhaps the old people were sellotaped to the sofas inside their granny flats and all the children banished to boarding school. Everyone is hidden away.

I'm hidden too!

Twelve

India

I couldn't believe it!

I had Treasure on my mind all through tea. I kept thinking of that horrible man and how he could hurt her. It made me feel so bad I couldn't eat much. I wouldn't really have fancied it anyway. It was one of Mum's special salads, a circle of cottage cheese in the centre of the plate, then a ring of pineapple, then carrot, cucumber and celery sticks like petals on a flower, then a fan of lettuce leaves either side, artistically arranged in shades of green and purple.

I nibbled the chunks of pineapple and left the rest.

'India? Why aren't you eating your salad?'

'I'm not hungry.'

Mum gave a silly laugh.

'Nonsense, darling, you're always hungry.'

'OK, OK, I'm always hungry,' I said. 'Only I just don't *happen* to be ravenous at this precise moment in time. And I doubt if a totally starving person would ever eat a mound of cottage cheese with gusto. Especially as it looks as if it's been eaten already and regurgitated by an anaemic alien.'

'That's enough, India! Less of the smart talk. Just eat!'

'For God's sake, leave the kid alone, Moya,' said Dad. 'She can't help it if she can't stick rabbit food.'

He gave me a significant wink to show me that *he* understood that pasta and ice-cream were my favourites. He wasn't making much headway with his own salad, though Mum allowed three slices of honey-glazed ham on his plate. It's a wonder she hadn't carved them into three little pink pigs.

We sat there, staring at our plates. Mum toyed with her own salad, eating with her fork in her right hand, American style, because she thinks it's more dainty. Wanda put her own fork down and asked if she could be excused as she was going out early with Suzi.

'Thank goodness,' said Mum, when Wanda was scarcely out of earshot. 'That girl is so *depressing*. I think we're going to have to get rid of her.'

I looked at Dad. He chewed his ham, his face carefully expressionless. Then he swallowed.

'Yes, she is a bit of a drag,' he said. 'See if you can find some kind way of sending her packing. Concern

130

for her health, shame that she's homesick, something along those lines.'

I couldn't believe it. He was betraying Wanda so casually. He didn't love her one little bit. He was bored with her so Mum was doing him a big favour. I felt so sorry for Wanda, even though *I* don't like her much either and don't really want her to stay.

'What *is* it, India?' Mum said.

I realized I'd been sighing. Dad looked at me anxiously.

'Nothing.'

'I do wish you'd buck up a bit. You seem so doleful recently. Bella says you've been writing really weird letters to Miranda.'

I felt my face flush as pink as Dad's ham.

'What do you mean, weird? And how does Bella know? Does Miranda show them to her?'

'Now now, calm down. Why do you always have to get in such a state about things? Miranda just happened to mention that you sounded rather lonely. You said you were missing her a great deal.'

'No I'm not. I don't miss her one little bit.'

'Oh, India. Typical! I've just been trying to fix up for us to have Miranda to stay one weekend.'

'Well you can unfix things, Mum, because I can't stick Miranda. I've got another friend now.'

I couldn't stop my tongue saying it. Mum looked up. Even Dad seemed interested. They both had their heads tilted to one side to indicate a question. I knew I couldn't give them any real answers.

'Come on then. Tell us about her. Do you want to invite her round for tea sometime?' said Mum.

'No!'

'Is she in your form at school?'

'Well . . .'

'What's her name?'

'Look, don't go *on* about her,' I said, and I got up and rushed out of the room.

I heard them talking about me as I went up the stairs.

'Oh dear, why does she always have to be so prickly?' said Mum. 'Do you think she's *really* got a friend at school at last?'

'That school! I simply can't manage those school fees any more.'

'Well, *I'll* pay them if it's such a problem – though I'm sure you're exaggerating all your financial difficulties.'

They started arguing about work and money and forgot all about me. I went upstairs and stared miserably out of my window. I thought about Anne. I love the passage in her diary where she says she can't bear her mother and wishes she could slap her. But Anne always loves her father and looks up to him so much. I suppose I still love my dad but I can't respect him any more.

I leant my forehead against the cold glass, looking down the long avenue. It looked pretty bleak, grey pavement, bare brown trees, cream stucco and beige brick houses – and a little flash of red. I stared. It was

Treasure! She was trudging along, her face white and screwed up, her fringe tangled, showing her ugly scar.

I tapped on the window. She couldn't hear me, wasn't even looking at my house. I struggled with the safety catch, wrenching my fingers. I got it open just as she was walking past.

'Treasure!' I hissed.

She spun round, head jerking to left and right.

'I'm up here!'

She looked up and spotted me.

'India!' she said joyfully.

'*Sh!*' I put my finger to my lips. 'Wait there! I'll be down in a sec.'

She stood still, waiting obediently. I gave her a little wave and then flew across my bedroom, crept along the landing, and edged down the stairs.

I didn't want Mum and Dad to meet Treasure. I knew exactly what they'd be like. They'd think they were being *sooo* nice. 'Oh, Treasure! What an unusual name! But *lovely*.'

'Where do you live, poppet? Oh, the Latimer Estate! I've heard they're really attractive flats once you get inside. They've got a lot of character – in their way.'

'So *you're* India's friend, are you? Well, you must come and play as often as you like. Don't feel shy, will you? You'll always be very welcome. Really.'

I knew what they'd say after she was gone too.

No, I was determined to keep Treasure all to myself. Mum and Dad were still busy rowing. They'd closed the dining-room door so I couldn't hear. That meant *they* couldn't hear me! I crept across the hall, opened the door, left it on the latch, and shot down the drive to Treasure.

'Treasure! This is so great! *I* went looking for you, but you weren't at your nan's. I saw him, your mum's boyfriend, and he's so scary!'

'You can say that again,' said Treasure. She tried to sound like she was joking but her voice wobbled.

'What's he done to you, Treasure?'

'Nothing this time. I got away. But he's still there, at Nan's. I can't go back. I can't . . .'

She started crying, though she kept wiping her eyes fiercely with her fists.

I put my arms round her. She was shivering inside her scarlet coat. She felt so *small*. She made me feel big and powerful. I knew I had to protect her. I had to save her from that hateful monster. I had to hide her.

And then it came to me.

It was so wondrously simple.

Treasure was like Anne Frank.

'Come with me, Treasure!' I said, tugging at her.

'I – I can't. I don't want to meet your mum, not like this. I look a mess,' said Treasure, sniffing and wiping.

'You're not going to meet her. You'd hate her anyway. No, you're coming with *me*. But keep quiet, eh?'

Treasure still looked doubtful, but she let me pull her up the drive and in through the door. She peered round the hall, her head swivelling.

'It's OK,' I whispered, nodding towards the closed

dining-room door. Dad and Mum were still at it. Dad said something and Mum suddenly yelled furiously. Treasure's mouth dropped open.

'Is that your mum?' she whispered. 'She's swearing!'

'She often does. She thinks it's cool,' I said scornfully. 'Come on.'

I took her by the hand and lead her up the stairs. Treasure peered round at all the paintings as if she was in a museum. She stopped when we got to the alabaster boy on his pedestal on the landing.

'Look at his little willy!' she giggled. She gave it a quick flick with her finger.

'Come *on*,' I said, pulling her past.

I took her up the stairs again.

'Your house is *huge*,' said Treasure. 'Which one's your bedroom?'

'It's that one, but I want you to—'

She wasn't listening. She peeped inside my bedroom and then just stood there, silent. Her eyes blinked rapidly behind her glasses.

'Oh India!' she gasped. It was as if all the breath had been sucked out of her.

'It's a bit of a mess,' I said quickly, shoving Edwina Bear under my pillow and kicking yesterday's socks and knickers under my bed.

'It's beautiful,' said Treasure.

She walked very carefully over to my bed, as if she was scared her trainers might mark the crimson carpet. It is a great bed, I suppose, like a four-poster in a fairy tale with black barley-sugar posts with little frogs carved on the top. It's got black satin hangings tied with crimson ribbons and a black satin patchwork quilt with little beads and buttons appliqued to each patch. It was my tenth birthday present. I thought it was pretty special at the time but now I suppose I've got used to it. There's a dressing-table too, black, with red lightbulbs all round the mirror, and each drawer has a tiny frog's head at either end of the handle.

Treasure glanced at herself in the mirror, wiped her nose quickly, and tried to flatten her fringe over her forehead. Then she walked over to the wardrobe. There are frogs carved into the black wood, hopping in spirals. Treasure traced them with her finger, looked at me for permission, and opened the wardrobe door. She stared at all the clothes stuffed inside. I wondered if she minded having to wear really tacky clothes like her red coat. I thought about offering her some of my stuff – but of course they'd all be too big.

I knew the clothes that *would* fit her.

'Come with me, Treasure,' I said.

I led her out of my room – though she kept looking back longingly – along the corridor to the attic steps. I clambered up, got the trapdoor open, and switched on the light. Treasure climbed after me, panting a little. I had to help haul her up.

She lay on the floor breathing heavily.

'Treasure? Treasure, are you all right?'

'It's just my asthma. I haven't got my inhaler. I dropped my bag when Terry came after me. Oh help!'

She sat up slowly, trying to take deep breaths. I patted her gently on the back to express sympathy. She wriggled away, giggling again.

'It's like I'm a baby being burped! I think I'm OK now. Have you got any pets, India? I'm a bit allergic to animals. Ha, that's why I can't stick Terry!'

'There's Tabitha, our old cat. But it's all right, she never comes up here. No-one does. That's the beauty of it! This can be *your* room, Treasure!'

She looked round at the clothes and the trunks and the boxes of books, bewildered.

'We'll fix it up. I'll bring all sorts of stuff. The armchair's quite comfy, I sit here myself sometimes. There's a camp bed, look, and a spare duvet – or you can have my pretty patchwork quilt if you like, I don't mind a bit.'

Treasure was walking slowly round the attic.

'What do you mean, it's my room?'

'You can hide here. It's a secret attic. You know, like Anne Frank.'

Treasure stared at me.

'But what about your mum and dad and this Wanda?'

'They won't ever find you. They never come up here. They don't notice a thing anyway. You can stay as long as you like, until that horrible man gives up and goes away.'

'Oh India, you're a true friend,' said Treasure, and she clasped my hands.

I squeezed her tightly back, so happy I wanted the

moment to last for ever. But I had to get busy getting Treasure settled for the night.

'I'll be right back,' I said, rushing off.

I hung over the landing to hear if Mum and Dad were still quarrelling. I wasn't sure when Wanda might get back either. I had to be quick.

I rushed all round my room, gathering bits here, bits there, frantically piling things into a pyramid on my carpet. It looked as if I'd have to rush up and down the attic steps again and again. Then I had a sudden sensible idea – I'd pack everything in my suitcase!

I managed to cram most things in. Then I had another thought. I grabbed my wastepaper bin too.

Treasure burst out laughing when I dragged everything up into the attic after me.

'You look like you're going on your holidays. Oh, and I've even got something for my rubbish!'

'Well, I thought you could use the wastepaper bin for . . . you know, when you have to go to the loo. I know it's not very nice, but Anne Frank and her family had to do it sometimes and they managed. I've got some tissues for you too.'

'Can't I use your toilet?' asked Treasure.

'Well, you can during the day, if Wanda's not around, or Mrs Winslow our cleaning lady, but you'll have to be very careful. And I've brought you some food, look.' I gave her my entire supply of chocolate and crisps and Coke, even though I was starving hungry after not eating my salad tea.

Treasure lined the chocolate bars up in a row,

touched the clean nightie and my thick Arran cardigan, looked at my drawing pad and crayons and then picked up the book I'd put there. *The Diary of Anne Frank*.

'I knew it!' she said, smiling. 'Well, I'll have to read it now, won't I?'

Thirteen

Treasure

India's so *kind*. She's the best friend in all the world. I'm sitting here wearing her posh nightie and her cuddly cardi, eating her chocolate, and I've already read fifty pages of her precious Anne Frank. She's in her secret annexe now. And so am I.

It doesn't seem real. India's acting like she's practised for this moment all her life. She's crept back twice this evening just to make sure I'm all right, and each time she's brought me more stuff. She even offered me her teddy bear. 'Though you probably think I'm an awful baby *having* a teddy bear. I just keep it for old time's sake. I don't *play* with her – it. Still, I thought it might make you feel cosy?'

I said it was very sweet of her but I didn't really

140

want her old teddy. I've never had my own teddy bear. I don't quite *get* why kids like them. I did have some Barbie dolls when I was little because they were cool with their pointy breasts and high heels and all their tiny adult outfits. Mum quite liked playing with them too. We'd play fashion models and famous actresses and Mum would give them all different voices and make them lark about.

It was great when I was little and it was just Mum and me.

No it wasn't. She mostly didn't want to play, she just wanted to lie back and smoke her roll-ups and drink and watch telly and if I pestered her she'd yell at me or give me a shove or a smack. She'd really lose it sometimes, telling me it was all my fault, if I hadn't been born she'd be out with her mates having fun instead of stuck at home night after night with a boring little brat like me.

Loretta is even younger than my mum was when I was born and she's stuck with Britney but she doesn't yell at her, she makes a big fuss of her. But Britney is pretty, with big blue eyes and lovely golden hair. She's so cute Nan thinks she should do a spot of modelling for magazines.

I've never been cute. I'm kind of ugly now but I was worse as a baby because one of my eyes was squinty and I had hardly any hair and eczema all over so I was scabby and cried a lot. Maybe it's not surprising my mum never went a bundle on me.

Nan always loved me though. When I was little I

stayed with Nan lots but then Mum got this boyfriend – not Terry, it was four or five blokes before him – and we moved up North because the houses were cheap but he couldn't get a job so that was a dead loss. All my mum's boyfriends have been awful. Sometimes they had kids but they didn't come and live with us too. It was always just Mum and me and the boyfriend until she took up with Terry. Then I had to get used to having Kyle and Bethany around all the time. Their mum had gone a bit mental on drugs so Terry got custody. If he could kid the court he was a fit father once I bet he could do it again.

He *is* quite a good dad to baby Gary, playing aeroplanes with him, whirling him up and down and making him whoop. He's OK with Kyle and Bethany too. He bought them both bikes and scooters and he acts the fool with them, wrestling with Kyle and tickling Bethany until she squeals. He's tried it with me too but I can't stand him pawing me about. So then he starts getting at me.

My own dad can't have thought much of me either because he pushed off the minute I was born. Well, who cares? *I've* pushed off now. I shall hang out here until . . . I don't know. I can't stay here for ever.

I'm so fussed about Nan. She'll be so worried about me. I'll have to try to let her know I'm OK.

I *am* OK. Though I wish I had my inhaler in case I get wheezy. My chest feels a bit tight. I could do with a drink but that's not a good idea. I'm trying to avoid going to the loo.

It's awful having to use India's wastepaper bin. It's so pretty too, black with pink roses to match her magical bedroom. I waited and waited, fidgeting, legs crossed, but eventually I had to give in and go. It was weirdly hard to get started even though I wanted to go so much, mostly because I couldn't sit properly, I just had to *hang* there. Once I got going I went so much I started to worry I wouldn't be able to stop. What if I carried on until the wee slopped right over the edge of the bin and flooded the floor? But it eased off eventually and the bin didn't get *too* full – though I won't be able to go all that often. And *what* am I going to do about the other thing? I shall die when India has to empty it.

I keep looking longingly at the bottle of Coke. I wish I hadn't eaten all that chocolate. I know it's India's secret supply. Am I going to have to live on chocolate all the time? I'd give anything for one of Nan's fry-ups. No, that's so ungrateful to poor India. I am lucky, lucky, lucky to have such a wonderful friend.

Fate was kind to us, letting India look out of her bedroom window just as I was going by.

That bedroom! I had no idea India's so *rich*. Her dad must earn millions. And her mum. I can't believe that she's really Moya Upton, the designer! I wonder if those are Moya Upton clothes in the corner?

They are *soooo* cool, the most wondrous clothes ever. India is MAD not to like them. I've just sorted all through them. I've tried heaps of them on. I hope India's mother won't mind. That is the most stupid thing I've ever written. She'd mind me hiding in her attic far more!

I particularly like some black trousers and a black top with a sequin rose. They fit me, even though I'm so small and skinny! I wish I had a mirror. Maybe I'll wear them tomorrow if India doesn't mind. I'm back in the nightie now. I should try to go to sleep. I don't feel tired though. I don't even want to sit for long. I feel like I want to keep running. I keep thinking about Terry.

I'll have to go back *some* time. And then he'll get me. It's like he's all Anne Frank's Gestapo rolled up into one monstrous man.

India's right about *The Diary of Anne Frank*. It's a great book. It starts off just like it's any girl's diary. She writes about her birthday presents and all the girls in her class, having a moan about most of them. Then she goes on about her boyfriends. That bit's irritating. But then suddenly she has to go into hiding and the whole story changes dramatically. Well, it isn't a story, it was her real life. I've looked at the last page. It has the worst possible end.

It's weird to think Anne Frank would be an old lady now if she'd managed to stay in hiding those few extra months until the end of the war. They stayed in the secret annexe more than two years.

I don't know how I'm going to manage two days. I'm so lonely. I wish India would come back. But this Wanda has come home now. I heard India say loudly, 'Oh *Wanda*, you're back already' – obviously

144

hoping I'd hear and realize I had to keep quiet now.

It is *soooo* quiet here. At least Anne had her sister and her parents and Peter and his family. I wouldn't even mind the grumpy old dentist. I just want someone to talk to. Anyone.

OK. I'll make someone.

There! I've used some of the Moya Upton clothes, stuffing T-shirts into a sweater and a pair of jeans so that they plump out as if someone is wearing them. I've rolled a T-shirt into a ball and stuck it on top of the sweater with a funny woolly hat on top. I've made a Clothes Person. I could call her Kitty, just like Anne Frank's imaginary friend.

Kitty is lucky. She doesn't need to go to the loo. I do.

She hasn't got any ears so she doesn't keep hearing footsteps.

She hasn't got a nose so she can't smell the waste bin.

She hasn't got any eyes so she can't see this spooky old attic. At least there is a light. I'm going to keep it on all the time, even when I'm asleep.

Only I *can't* sleep. I don't have a watch but I think it must be the middle of the night. I heard two people go to the bathroom one after the other, India and Wanda. The water tank gurgled and splashed later on. I think her parents used their bathroom on the first floor. No-one's moved around for ages now. I've read another hundred pages of Anne Frank. I've drawn a special thank-you card for India, with a picture of the two of us, hugging. I had to have several attempts. The first time I drew India too big and I was worried it would upset her. The second time I coloured my scar in too vigorously so it looked like Terry had hacked my head in two. So it was third time lucky, and when I'd coloured us in more carefully this time, I enclosed us in a red heart and drew multi-coloured daisies to fill up the rest of the page. Then in my very best nearly-italic writing I wrote: *To India, the Best Friend in all the World.*

She will like it a lot, I know. I felt good all the time I was drawing my picture. Not quite so lonely. But now I feel bad again. And maybe it's silly to say India is my best friend because I've only known her a little while. I don't know much about her. I still feel a bit shy with her sometimes, not cosy like I do with Patsy.

I wish I could cuddle up with Patsy now.

No, I wish I could cuddle up with Nan.

Oh, Nan.

Oh, Nan.

Oh, Nan.

I don't think I went to sleep until it was nearly morning. I woke with a terrible start when the trap-door opened. I didn't know where I was. I covered my head in case it was Terry coming to get me. But of course it was India, carefully balancing a proper breakfast tray one-handed.

I feel so mean moaning that I might have to live on chocolate. This is what she brought me for breakfast:

a bowl of cornflakes with brown sugar and sliced bananas and milk, two slices of toast, one with honey, one with apricot jam, a saucer of strawberries, a glass of fresh orange juice, and a cup of tea.

'I've spilt half the tea,' she said sadly.

'It's perfect! Wonderful. Thanks ever so much, India.'

I looked at the big silver shiny thing she'd tucked under one arm. 'Is that a *saucepan* lid?'

India went pink. 'It's Mum's biggest wok lid. I was thinking about the bin, you see.' She went over to the waste bin in the corner, delicately averting her eyes, and dropped the lid on top. It fitted snugly.

'There! I just thought it would be nicer and easier when I empty it. Which I'll do now, while everyone's still asleep.'

So I sat back like Little Lady Muck and ate my beautiful breakfast while poor India trundled off with the sloppety bin. Goodness knows how she got it down those steps without dropping it. She brought it back all fresh and smelling of Toilet Duck.

She stayed for a long time too, both of us in our nightclothes. We were suddenly just like two girls having a sleepover party. We mucked about and got the giggles (stifled) and played silly paper games like noughts and crosses and hangman and battleships. I've always been heaps better than anyone else at paper games (there's no point playing Patsy because I *always* win) but India is a challenge.

I did beat her twice though – and she didn't guess my hangman word though I was sure she would:

SECRET ANNEXE. Then she wanted to challenge me to an Anne Frank quiz but it was obvious who would win. We both drew her instead. We chose our favourite photo from the diary and copied it. India's was neater, with a border of little checked diaries and pens, and she managed a better likeness too. India politely said my drawing was much better than hers, but we both knew she was fibbing.

'I wish I looked like Anne,' said India, stroking the photo. 'Hasn't she got the most beautiful eyes ever? She looks so intelligent, don't you think?'

'Yeah, but I don't like her hair much. Why did she have to curl it like that? I think she'd look much better with straight hair, and longer, past her shoulders. I wish I had long hair. You're lucky, India.' I pulled one of her fuzzy plaits.

'I *hate* my hair. I'd much sooner have soft floppy hair like yours. I love the way your fringe goes. It looks cute.'

She patted it – and I winced automatically.

'Oh, God, I'm sorry! Is your cut still sore?'

'No, not really, not a bit.'

India gently parted my fringe and looked at the scar.

'How could he, Treasure?' she whispered.

'You should see what he's done to my mum. He broke her jaw, he knocked out two teeth, he punched her in the stomach when she was expecting little Gary—'

'Then why on earth does she *stay* with him?' India asked, looking astonished.

'Well . . . she loves him.'

'You can't love someone who *punches* you.'

'Yes you can, if you're stupid, like my mum. He goes all smarmy afterwards and he cries and swears it will never happen again. She's mad enough to believe it.'

'I still don't get it,' said India, shaking her head. 'No-one could believe him.'

India gets it now! This afternoon she came back with a PORTABLE TELEVISION!

'Well, it seemed like a good idea. Wanda's out and Dad's asleep and Mum's gone to her workshop so no-one will ever know,' said India, out of breath from lugging it up the stairs.

'You'll be carrying your entire *bedroom* up here soon,' I said. 'Still, what a great idea!'

India switched it on and fiddled about until she got a programme.

'Ah, the news,' I said. 'Wonder if I'm on it, eh?'

I was joking – but I WAS!

There was a piece about a politician, then something about the countryside, all the usual boring stuff, but then suddenly there was a photo of *me* right above the newsreader's head.

'It's me, India, look!'

'That's not you!' said India, though they were reading my name out right that minute.

She didn't recognize me because it was an ages-old photo, from nearly two years ago when I was a little kid. We were on holiday at the seaside, Mum and me, and although I'm little I look bigger in the photo, all bouncy and smiley with my hair scooped up in silly little bunches. And there with his hand on my shoulder, giving me a hug, is Terry the Torturer. The horrible thing is, I'm looking up at him with this stupid grin on my face. We'd just met up with him and his kids and he was making this big fuss of my mum and me, taking us on all the rides at the funfair and treating us to pizzas and fish and chips and ice-cream. Every time he bought Kyle and Bethany any game or T-shirt or baseball cap he bought me one too. I fell for him just as heavily as Mum, even though I'm meant to be the bright one.

I *hate* that photo. The newsreader said that I'd been missing twenty-four hours. There's been a big police search but so far no-one has spotted me – though there are unconfirmed reports of my going off with some *man*.

'I wouldn't go off with any man! Are they nuts?' I said.

'It's just like when Anne and her family went into hiding. There were all these rumours that they'd gone here, there and everywhere. People swore they'd seen them.'

'Sh! Look! Oh God!'

They were showing Nan's flat – but she was edged right into a corner. You could just see a strand of her fair hair and a bit of her shoulder as she sat on the arm of the sofa. My mum was right in the middle, holding baby Gary, with Terry beside her, his arm round them both. Mum was crying. *Terry* was crying too, his green eyes spilling tears.

'We're so worried about our Treasure,' he said, straight to camera. His voice was husky with emotion. 'Please come home, darling – if you can.'

Mum burst into fresh floods and Terry pulled her closer, all tender concern.

I wanted to *vomit*.

Fourteen

India

I can't believe that awful scary Terry could seem so heartbroken. He is brilliant at acting. It was so strange seeing Treasure's family on television. They interviewed a senior police officer who said they were becoming increasingly concerned for Treasure's safety. He urged the public to come forward if they had seen her. But no-one at all can see her – except me!

It's so extraordinary. All the police are out searching for her when all the time Treasure's safe and sound in my secret attic.

Well, she's *safe*. I'm not sure about sound. She isn't very well today. She's worrying about her nan so she's all tense and that makes her chest tight and she gets asthma. When it's bad she wheezes in-between words as if she's a little old lady. She needs her inhaler but she's lost her bag. There's a spare inhaler at her nan's though.

'Can't you go and see her after school, India?' Treasure begged. 'You could get her on her own and whisper where I am. She won't tell. You can trust my nan. And then she can slip you my spare inhaler.'

'But what if Terry and your mum are still there? If they see me again they might start to get really suspicious. It's too risky.'

Treasure sighed wheezily. She sat all hunched up, her fists clenched as she fought for breath.

'Try to relax, Treasure. Straighten your shoulders and take deep breaths.'

'I – *can't* – breathe – you – nut,' she gasped.

I massaged her shoulders and back, talking to her all the time, telling her to breathe *in* and *out*, *in* and *out*—

'Shut – up – you – berk,' said Treasure.

But it was helping! She was soon breathing almost normally.

'How did you know what to do?'

'I think maybe I saw some stuff on *Casualty*,' I admitted.

'Do you want to be a nurse then?'

'Well, I want to be a writer, like Anne. But I wouldn't mind being a doctor. No, a surgeon, I'd like that, cutting people open and doing complicated operations. I'm not a bit squeamish.'

'Just as well when you have to empty my horrible bin,' said Treasure, shuddering.

'I don't mind,' I said.

Well, it is pretty revolting actually, but I can manage. Wanda saw me coming out of the bathroom carrying the emptied bin and stared in astonishment.

'Why have you got the bin and a *saucepan* lid?' she said.

'It's . . . personal,' I said.

Wanda looked a little embarrassed.

'Oh! I see,' she said, and disappeared into the bathroom herself.

I heard her being sick. I hoped she hadn't got some bug. I didn't want Treasure to get it. I told her when I nipped up the attic steps. Treasure looked at me as if I was stupid.

'She could have a tummy bug, *or* she could be going to have a baby,' she said.

It was like an alarm bell going off inside my brain. I couldn't bear it. Treasure thought I was shaking my head because I didn't believe her.

'I don't know, of course. It's just my mum threw up a lot when she was pregnant with Gary. India?' Treasure knelt down beside me.

'She's been acting all worried for weeks. She hasn't been eating properly either. I think she *is* pregnant.'

'But why are you getting so het up about it?'

'I think it's my dad's baby!'

Treasure blinked at me. 'Oh! I *see*.'

'It's awful. He doesn't even like her much. He wants to get rid of her. But maybe now she's having his baby he'll change his mind? Maybe he'll go off with Wanda?'

'I don't think he'll leave all this,' said Treasure, looking around to indicate our house. 'Not unless Wanda is really, really gorgeous.'

'She isn't,' I said sadly. I thought about my dad, my mum, Treasure's mum, Terry . . .

'I hate grown ups,' I said bitterly. 'You can't trust any of them.'

'They're not all like that,' said Treasure. 'You can trust my nan.'

She wheezed again.

'Breathe, Treasure. Don't tighten up,' I said quickly. 'Look, I'll phone her. How about that?'

'Can't I phone her?' Treasure said eagerly.

'Well, I could try and sneak you Mum or Dad's mobile. I'll do my best when I get back from school, OK?'

'Don't go,' Treasure said, gripping my arm. 'Stay here with me, India, please.'

'I'd give anything to stay, you know I would, but I *can't*. Wanda drives me to school. I'll have to whizz off in a minute. Well, kind of *now*.' I tried very gently to unhook Treasure's hands.

'It's so lonely up here,' she said. 'Can't I come out during the day?'

'It's a bit risky, Treasure.'

'But your mum and dad will be out at work.'

'Wanda will be here though. She does go out some-times, shopping, or to a yoga class, but you'll never be able to guess when she'll be back. No, stay up here. I wish *I* could. You've got all the books and my drawing stuff – and you've got your lunch all waiting.'

I'd tried really hard with Treasure's lunch, making her cheese salad sandwiches and tuna and sweetcorn rolls with carrot sticks and tomatoes and a cherry yoghurt and a flapjack and an apple and a bottle of orange juice. I heard Mum's high-heeled boots tapping down the stairs so I shoved the lot into my schoolbag in the nick of time. Mum looked at me suspiciously, asking why I'd gone pink. She tutted when she saw the bag of brown rolls was open.

'Have you been at those baps, India? How many have you eaten? You *know* you're only supposed to have muesli and fruit for breakfast. It's for your own good.' She went on at me, nag, nag, niggle, niggle, while she brewed her black coffee and nibbled a single slice of melon.

I was happy to let her think I was this great greedy pig but I wished Treasure might act a *little* pleased. She hadn't eaten her breakfast either, not one bite, though I'd tried hard to vary it, toast and honey, melon cocktail, a banana and a carton of milk.

'Eat your breakfast, Treasure,' I said. 'I've *got* to go now. I'll try hard to see your nan after school, I promise, and I'll come rushing back home as quick as quick after that. The day will just flash by, you'll see.'

Treasure nodded, but she was nibbling her lip anxiously. I gave her a quick hug. I didn't like leaving her, but what else could I do?

It was so strange to run downstairs and start off for school as if nothing had happened. I felt awkward with Wanda. I kept giving her tummy little glances as she drove me to school, imagining a tiny tadpole baby swimming about inside her. I wanted to know if it was really true but I went hot at the thought of asking her.

'You're very quiet,' said Wanda, as she drew up outside school.

'Yes, well, I've got things on my mind,' I said.

'Me too,' said Wanda significantly. 'Anyway, I'll pick you up usual time this afternoon. Don't worry, I won't be late.'

'No! We've got our arrangement, don't you remember? I'm coming home by myself.'

'I've changed my mind, India. It's not safe. That kid's still missing from the Latimer Estate. They think some man's abducted her.'

'That's rubbish,' I said. 'I bet she's just run away.'

'Whatever,' said Wanda. 'I'm still coming to pick you up.'

'No, you're not,' I said. 'I'm going to my friend Tiffany's house. And then her mum will drive me home. It's all arranged.'

'Does your mother know?'

'No. I don't want to tell her. You know what she's like.'

'Yes,' said Wanda. 'But I still think—'

'Wanda, I've got to go, I'm *late*.'

I was out of the car and running into school before she could continue.

It was a trying day at school. Maria and Alice had some new joke together, nudging each other and giggling whenever they looked in my direction. I kept dropping the wretched ball in PE. The whole class groaned and went, 'Surprise, surprise' when I came top in the Maths test. It was pizza for lunch but my slice was very small and burnt underneath.

I didn't really care about any of this. School suddenly seemed such a stupid trivial place. I hurtled across the playground the second the bell went for home-time just in case Wanda was thinking of collecting me after all. I was way down the road while the others had scarcely started straggling across the playground.

I ran nearly the whole way to the Latimer Estate, rehearsing what I was going to say to Treasure's nan. But I didn't get the chance.

There were two big television vans parked in the courtyard of Elm block and over by the dustbin shelter there was a crowd clustered in front of the television camera. Kids were running towards it, desperate to be on television too. I grabbed one little boy by his bony elbow.

'What's going on?'

'Leave off! It's the telly, innit. They've got the bloke.'

'Which bloke?'

'The one that murdered the girl, Treasure.'

'She's not murdered!'

'Well, they haven't found her body yet, but my mum says it's only a matter of time. She says they should torture him until he says what he's done with her.'

'*Who?*'

'That nutter Michael Watkins. He's the one that did it.'

'Michael Watkins?'

'You are *thick*. He lives next door to Treasure and her gran, Rita, and all that crowd.'

Mumbly Michael!

'He hasn't done anything to Treasure!'

'Yes, he has. The coppers came and arrested him. They did a search of his mum's flat and all. There's no trace of Treasure – *yet*. My mum reckons they should search the dustbins. She'll be found soon, you wait.'

He jerked his elbow free and ran towards the television crew. I ran after him, though my legs were so wobbly I nearly fell down.

They *couldn't have* arrested poor Mumbly Michael.

They could.

A journalist was talking solemnly straight to camera.

'We understand that the police are still questioning this man, who is believed to be the next-door neighbour of Treasure Mitchell's grandmother. There's still no sign of the little girl herself but her family haven't given up hope.'

I wondered if this *family* were still staying with Nan in her flat. I skirted the crowd and dodged up the stairs, but when I got to the right landing I saw

159

there were two police officers outside Nan's flat, and two more outside Mumbly Michael's.

I felt so frightened I just bobbed back down the stairs, rushing too quickly in the dark. I missed my footing and went hurtling down four or five steps at once, landing with a terrible thump on my hands and knees, my schoolbag giving me another bash in the back for good measure. I knelt there, whispering all the swear words I know to try to stop myself crying. Then I picked myself up and limped down the rest of the stairs.

The television crew was still filming, the camera panning the crowd. I kept my head well down and backed away. I ran until I was out of the Latimer Estate altogether, and then I hobbled along to the parade of shops. I went to the chemist's. I had ten pounds in my school purse. I hoped it would be enough. I smiled at the lady behind the counter.

'Can I have one of those asthma inhaler things, please?'

'Have you got your prescription, dear?'

Oh-oh.

'No, I've been very stupid. I've lost it. Couldn't you just give me the inhaler? I can pay, I've got my money.'

'No dear, you have to have the prescription. You'll have to go back to your doctor.'

'I can't. I haven't got an appointment. I need the inhaler now. I'm going off to stay at a friend's, you see, and I'm starting to go all wheezy.'

I started to imitate Treasure having an attack. It was quite easy because I was still out of breath from all the running.

'I'm sorry, we're not allowed to sell any asthma products over the counter without a prescription,' she said.

'Look, can't you give the inhaler to me now, and I'll use it and calm down and go and see the doctor and get another prescription and bring it straight back to you, I promise.'

'No, I'm afraid that's just not possible.' She was staring at me, starting to get suspicious. 'Are you on your own? Is your mother outside in the car?'

'Oh, never mind,' I said, giving up and running out of the shop. I hoped the television and newspapers hadn't said anything about Treasure being asthmatic. I decided to trail all the way into town to see if I could buy anything for asthma at the big Boots in the shopping centre. I thought I'd seem much less conspicuous in a crowded shop. I just hoped they had a different policy.

They didn't. They wouldn't sell me an inhaler. They went through the whole we-need-a-prescription rigmarole. So I gave up and spent the ten pounds on treats for Treasure instead: blue sparkly nail varnish and cherry-flavoured lip gloss and butterfly slides and some chocolate – and I bought room freshener too and more tissues.

It was getting horribly late now. I knew Treasure would be wondering where on earth I'd got to. I ran some of the way home but I was tired out and my knees were hurting badly so I wasn't very fast.

I wanted to rush straight up to Treasure but Wanda was waiting in the hall.

'This isn't good enough, India! Why didn't you ring me from Tiffany's house? I've been so worried.'

'There's no *need* to worry, Wanda.'

Wanda was still looking at me strangely. 'There's something going on, India. You're acting very oddly all of a sudden.' She paused. 'You didn't slip back here at lunchtime, did you?'

I felt my heart thump. I tried not to look anxious. 'No. Why?'

'Mrs Winslow seemed sure someone had been in the kitchen.'

'Oh?' I said, as if I wasn't that interested. 'Anyway, Wanda, I'd better go and get started on my homework, I've got heaps.'

I raced upstairs and made a great show of slamming my bedroom door – and then I opened it again very cautiously, scooted along the landing, and up the stairs.

I poked my head up into the attic. It was pitch black!

'Treasure? What is it? What's happened?'

I felt for the light switch. I found it but the light didn't come on.

'Treasure?'

Why wasn't she answering me?

I pulled myself up and felt my way in the darkness.

'Treasure, please! It's me, India. Where are you?'

162

I found the armchair but it was empty. Then I nudged into something on the floor. I bent and felt clothes, a limp body, arms, legs. I shook her gently – and to my horror her arm came right off, dangling there in my hands!

Fifteen

Treasure

It's been the longest day ever, ever, ever.

I ate my breakfast. By ten o'clock I'd eaten my lunch too, just for something to do. Then I felt sick and started to worry what I would do if I *was* sick. I wasn't sure how much that horrible wastebin would hold. And how could I be sick without making a noise? Wanda might hear, unless she was too busy being sick herself. Fancy India not guessing she's pregnant. India seems so grown-up and she uses all these la-di-da long words but she's like a little kid really. Our Patsy knows more than she does.

I mustn't think about Patsy. Or any of the family. I might start fussing and have an asthma attack. I'm still a bit wheezy. I'm trying to breathe slowly and calmly

164

but when you *think* about breathing you forget how to do it properly. I can't help wondering what will happen if I have a really *bad* asthma attack, like the time Mum had that terrible row with the neighbours when she lived with Big Bill. They set their dog on her and I screamed and then I couldn't stop, I couldn't catch my breath, I was just *gasp gasp gasp*. Mum had to get me to hospital quick. I always needed my inhaler after that.

I need it now.

I do so, so, so hope India goes to see Nan.

I *mustn't* think about Nan. I'll think about . . . Anne Frank. I've read her whole diary now. It gets harder towards the end but you keep on reading because you care about her so much. You wonder what she's going to do with Peter too, though he's far too dull and boring for Anne.

She never got the chance to meet anyone else. The diary doesn't finish the way you want it to, with the war ending and Holland liberated and Anne and her family and all the other Jews free to come out of hiding and all the concentration camps opened up and everyone nursed back to full health. The diary stops and then there are a couple of pages telling you what happens next, if you can bear to read it.

I wonder what it felt like to be stuck in that awful camp?

I wonder if Anne knew she was going to die?

I wonder what it was like to be one of the guards, maybe with his own teenage daughters at home?

I don't get why people *want* to hurt other people. I don't get why Terry wants to hurt me. I don't get why my mum loves Terry even though he hurts her. If I ever win the Lottery I'm going to buy a great big house – maybe one like this – and it'll just be for really *special* people. Nan. India, if she wants. Patsy. Loretta and little Britney. Maybe Willie can hang out with us too. My mum can come, but only if she promises not to bring any blokes with her. Especially not Terry.

It'll be my house and my rules and the minute anyone hits or hurts or gets drunk or shoots up they're *out*, no arguments, immediate eviction.

I'll draw the house . . .

OK, I've done the house and I've given everyone their own room. There are *no* attics, secret or otherwise. I have seen enough attics to last me a lifetime.

I got so fed up by one o'clock and so *hungry* too, wishing I hadn't gobbled up all my lunch long ago. I wondered about risking slipping downstairs. I lay down and put my ear to the trapdoor and listened. I couldn't hear a thing.

I'd heard Wanda come in once, and then she'd gone out again about quarter to one. I was sure she couldn't have crept back. So I opened up the trapdoor and slipped down the stairs, trembling. I listened on the landing. I felt like I had great flappy elephant ears I was listening so hard.

The house was silent. Well, a tap dripped, a clock ticked, the radiators gurgled, but there was no human noise. I ran along the landing to the bathroom. It was bliss, bliss, bliss to use a proper toilet. I had a wash and cleaned my teeth too. I hoped India wouldn't mind me using her things.

I went and had another peep in her bedroom, marvelling. I'd wondered if I'd made half of it up, but it was even better than I'd remembered. I stroked the quilt on the fairytale bed and rubbed my cheek against the smooth silky pillow. I longed to climb into the bed and curl up and sleep.

I can't sleep properly all by myself up in that attic. I wriggled around all night on that tiny camp bed. Every time I started dozing Terry came stalking me, his green eyes gleaming as he undid his leather belt. I'd feel safe in India's soft bed but if I fell asleep I might not wake up in time. Wanda might come back and find me.

I checked on Wanda's bedroom. There were a lot of screwed-up tissues on her pillow. It looked like she'd been crying for hours. She was obviously very upset about the baby. Loretta was pleased she had Britney. She said a baby is someone of your very own to love. She certainly loves Britney lots. Maybe Wanda's worried what her mum and dad in Australia will think. Nan cried when Loretta told her she was going to have a baby. She said she wasn't mad, she was sad, because Loretta was still such a kid herself. Nan thought Loretta should have waited, finished school, done some training, *made* something of herself.

'I've made a baby instead,' said Loretta.

'You girls,' said Nan. 'Maybe it's my fault. What's the matter with me, eh? First it's Tammy, expecting at seventeen, and now it's you.'

'I'm not like Tammy,' said Loretta. 'She never wanted hers.'

Nan shushed her, but I heard. It didn't come as any surprise. I know my mum never wanted me.

She didn't even want to hold me when I was born. She told me. I was all purple and slimy so she couldn't stand the sight of me. The nurse bathed me and powdered me and brushed my hair and popped me into a pink sleeping suit. I've seen a photo. I didn't look too bad. One of my eyes looks a bit wonky but I'm sort of cute otherwise, with this fluff all over my head like a dandelion.

'Look at your little baby, your little treasure,' said this kind nurse. 'Don't you want to give her a cuddle?'

'I'd sooner give her a clip round the head for all the pain she caused me,' my mum moaned. 'My little *treasure*?'

She said it as a joke. She used it as my nickname. So that's what I got called. I don't care if she didn't mean it in a nice way.

Well, I do care. But it's OK, my mum loves me now. She wants me back. She was *crying* on the television.

Oh, come off it. That doesn't mean anything. *Terry* was crying too.

I wish they'd shown my nan on the telly.

There was a phone in the kitchen. I dialled 141 so the call couldn't be traced and then punched in Nan's number. It was answered at the first ring. It wasn't Nan.

It was Terry!

'Hello?' he said into my ear. 'Hello, hello? Who's that? Look if it's one of you journalists playing silly beggars I've *told* you, we've got an exclusive with another paper.'

There was another voice telling Terry to hand the phone over – maybe a policeman? Than I heard Nan!

'Shut up! It could be Treasure. Let me speak to her! Treasure? Is it you, darling? Are you all right? Where *are* you?'

'I'm hiding, Nan!' I whispered, and then I put the phone down quick in case someone else snatched it.

My throat was dry. I poured myself a glass of water. My hands were so shaky I spilt half of it down my front. I wandered round the huge kitchen seeing little bug-eyed Treasures in every shiny surface. What would Nan think of a kitchen like this! The fridge had all sorts of fancy food but I didn't dare help myself. The larder was easier. I had a handful of raisins, a licked finger of sugar, and then I got started on a packet of cornflakes. They made me cough. Then I started wheezing. I put my hands on my tight chest and told myself to take it e–a–s–y – but then I saw a dark shape through the mottled glass of the kitchen door, and the sound of a key in the lock!

I ran like the wind, out of the kitchen, up the two flights of stairs, up the attic ladder and through the trapdoor. I lay on the floor of the attic, gasping. Blood drummed in my head. It was so loud I couldn't hear properly. Oh God, there were footsteps! Coming along the landing, getting nearer and nearer.

'Come out!' someone called. An oldish voice. 'I heard you! I'll call the police!'

I lay there, my hand over my mouth. I heard the ladder creaking. They were coming up after me!

I reached out and found the light switch. I flicked it off quickly and lay still in the dark. I hate not being able to see but it meant *they* wouldn't be able to see me if they stuck their head through the trapdoor.

It was opening! I clamped my lips together, in agony.

'Are you in there? It's not you, is it, India?'

I waited for her to work out where the light switch was.

'India?' she said again, but with less conviction. She sighed – and then went back down the ladder, pausing to put the trapdoor back in place. I heard her down on the landing, muttering to herself.

I waited until I heard distant hoovering. I sat up, wheezing, and switched the light back on. I kept telling myself that it was OK, she hadn't found me. But I couldn't stop feeling scared.

I'm still scared. If only India would come back! I need my inhaler. I can't breathe. It's getting worse.

Footsteps. India? But what if it's the cleaning lady? I'd better switch the light off quick.

*   *   *

I tried to switch the light back on but the light bulb's broken! I'm in the dark. I'm so scared. I'm trying to write this but I can't see what I'm doing.

The footsteps went away ages ago. Where's India? It must be so late now. Maybe it's night-time already?

I want Nan. Did she hear me? Does she know I'm all right? But I'm not all right. I'm getting so scared. I can't breathe. *Ican'tbreatheIcan'tbreatheIcan'tbreathe.*

Sixteen

India

Dear Kitty

I bet I've kept you on tenterhooks!

I screamed as Treasure fell apart in my arms.

'Treasure!'

'I'm here – I – can't – breathe!'

I felt my way towards her. I'd been holding the clothes doll she'd made for company! The real Treasure was huddled up in a corner of the black attic. She clutched hold of me.

'Have – you – got – my—'

'Your inhaler? No, I *tried*. I've been everywhere. But it's OK, Treasure, I'll help you breathe.'

Treasure sucked in a breath and then said something very rude. I didn't think she was being fair. I'd

172

tried so hard. But I held her and straightened her shoulders in the dark and after a bit she stopped wheezing so much. She started telling me about going downstairs and nearly being caught by Mrs Winslow – I *told* her not to come out the attic! – and the light bulb going and how she panicked in the dark and then passed out. I felt she might just have gone to sleep but I didn't like to contradict her.

I gave her the bag of presents and told her to feel each one and see if she could tell what it is while I nipped downstairs and tried to find a new light bulb. She didn't want me to go and leave her alone in the dark again.

'I'll just be a minute, I promise,' I said – but I got waylaid.

Wanda was in her bedroom, so I helped myself to all sorts of stuff in the kitchen, including a 100 watt light bulb. I shoved everything on a tray and started carrying it upstairs. But Dad suddenly came bursting through the front door, home from work a good hour early.

'How's my little girl then?' he called up the stairs after me. He sounded friendly for once but there was something odd about his voice. It was thicker, as if he was getting a cold.

'Hi, Dad,' I said, and carried on up the stairs.

'Hey, hey! Come and give your old dad a kiss then!'

I tried blowing him one, balancing the tray against my chest.

'I want a proper hello hug!' Dad insisted, bounding

173

up the stairs after me. He tripped and went, 'Whoopsie,' sounding foolish.

He wasn't getting a cold. He was drunk. It was obvious when he caught me up. He smelt awful and his eyes were bleary and bloodshot. What was he *doing*, drinking at work?

I gave his cheek a hasty kiss and tried to edge round him.

'Come here, India. You love your old dad no matter what, don't you, darling?'

'Yes Dad,' I said – though I'm not sure I do now.

He tried to hug me and the tray tipped.

'Careful, Dad, please.'

'What's all this then?' said Dad, stirring all the food with his forefinger. He wagged it at me.

'Naughty, naughty! I thought your sainted stick-thin mother had put you on a diet?'

'It's just a little snack for when I'm doing my homework.'

'Won't the light bulb taste a bit crunchy?' said Dad, roaring with laughter at his own feeble joke.

'Oh ha ha, Dad. Please. Let me go and get on with my homework,' I said.

Dad tagged after me all the way to my room.

'Dad! Look, you can't come in here, it's private,' I said desperately.

'I've got to fix your light bulb, darling. Can't have my little sweetheart electrocuting herself.' Dad switched on my bedroom light and stared stupidly at the three glowing bulbs. He tried to snap his fingers.

'Abracadabra! Fixed already!'

'No, Dad, the light bulb's for – for school. I've got to take it for Science tomorrow.'

Thank goodness that diverted him.

'That bloody school. They charge a small fortune – no, no, a *huge* fortune – in fees, and now they want your old dad to fork out for light bulbs!' He started a long rant about my school and how he didn't have any money at *all*. He even got out his wallet and flapped it in my face to show me it was empty.

He was getting really angry. It was as if my real dad had been abducted by aliens and they'd sent this mad mean replicant dad in his place.

'Dad, you're *scaring* me.'

He blinked at me. His face screwed up. 'No, *I'm* the one who's scared,' he said. 'I'm in such a mess.'

'Oh, Dad. It's Wanda, isn't it?' I whispered.

'Wanda?' said Dad. 'What's Wanda got to do with it? What's she been saying to you?'

'Nothing! Don't talk about her like that, Dad, please.'

'I'll talk about her how I want,' said Dad, his voice thickening. 'It's my house, isn't it?' He missed a beat. 'Well, no, tell a lie, it's not my house at all. It's your mother's house, it's *her* name on the mortgage. How about that to make a man feel small? Still, just as well, I suppose, given the circumstances.'

I didn't know what he was talking about. His voice tailed off as he lost his thread. He shook his head and then belched.

'You're drunk, Dad.'

'Good! Well, I intend to get drunker,' he said. He turned on his heel and lurched down the landing.

I listened to him going downstairs, wondering if he'd miss his footing and fall headlong. I wanted him to.

I don't know how much Wanda heard. She came scurrying along to my room right away.

'What's your dad doing home from work so early?'

I shrugged. 'Don't ask me. He shouldn't have been driving home. He's drunk.'

'Oh dear.' Wanda looked stricken. 'I'd better go to him.'

'I'd leave him alone if I were you. He's in a foul mood,' I said.

Wanda took no notice. She went downstairs – and I risked rushing *up* the steps to the attic, balancing the tray. Treasure was in a state again, but when I'd got the new light bulb screwed in – jolly difficult in the pitch dark – she calmed down. She had a long drink of orange juice and then started picking at one of my special sandwiches, banana, cream cheese and honey. She poked the bits of banana out and licked the honey.

'Eat it properly, Treasure!' I said.

I munched my own sandwich with appropriate appreciation. I ended up eating most of Treasure's too.

'Why were you so *long*, India?'

'My dad got hold of me. He's drunk. He's so *disgusting*.'

'You mean he's been down the pub?'

'I don't know. He has these secret bottles of whisky. He keeps one in his desk here. Maybe he's got one in his desk at work too. I hate the smell of him when he's been drinking whisky.'

'I hate the smell too. And the way it makes them so mean. Terry would always go for me when he'd had a few whiskies,' said Treasure, rubbing her forehead.

'He hit you other times?'

'Lots! One time he thought I was sneering at him for something and he got his hand round my throat and I thought he was going to kill me. He said it was just a joke to teach me a lesson but he left bruise marks all round my neck and Mum had to keep me off school. He bought me a stupid big bear with wobbly eyes and a little heart saying "MAKE FRIENDS" after. He tried to get round me, pretending to *be* the bear, talking in this stupid growly voice. I just sat stone-faced and Mum said I was a hard-hearted little cow and couldn't I see Terry was doing his best to make it up to me.'

'That's so mean of your mum!'

'She's like that. She can't seem to help it. She'd forgive him anything just because he's her bloke. He could cut my throat and she'd go, "Oh, Treasure, don't bleed to death, you mean cow, now you'll get Terry into trouble with the cops." Hey, wouldn't it be incredible if the cops thought Terry had done away with me now! We could phone up anonymously and say we're sure Treasure Mitchell's dead and it's all down to her dodgy stepdad, last seen chasing her down an alleyway in Latimer!' Treasure was chortling with laughter in spite of her wheezy chest. Then she saw my face.

'What is it? He *hasn't* been arrested, has he?'

'He hasn't – but Michael has.'

'Michael? What do you mean? Which Michael?'

'The funny one with the mum, next door to your Nan.'

'Old Mumbly Michael! Goodness, what's he done? He wouldn't hurt a fly.'

'They think he's hurt you.'

'*What?* Are they nuts? Why *Michael*? He helped me hide from Terry. Oh God. Maybe someone saw me with Michael? Oh, India, what are we going to do? His mum will be going spare. Michael won't even understand. This is so awful!'

'I know – but I'm sure they'll let him go after they've questioned him.'

'What if they don't?' Treasure took hold of my arm. 'Do you think I ought to give myself up?'

'No! No, you mustn't, of course you mustn't.'

'Why did it all have to go so wrong? I was so happy at Nan's,' Treasure wailed.

I couldn't help feeling wounded. Why couldn't she be happy *here*? I'd tried so hard to make her welcome and comfort her and give her treats. I didn't say a word but Treasure saw my face.

'I'm sorry, India,' she said. 'You've been so lovely to me. I'm ever so grateful, honestly. It's just that I wish I could go *home*. I can't ever be safe with Nan while Terry's around. He's going to get me eventually, I just

know he is and I don't know what to *do*!' Treasure
punched the floorboards violently.

'Don't! They might hear. And you'll hurt yourself,
silly. *And* start up your asthma.'

'How am I going to manage without my inhaler?'

'You'll manage fine.'

'It was so scary when I was up here in the dark. I
couldn't breathe at all.'

'But you're OK now.'

'I'm wheezing.'

'Only a little tiny bit. You just need to sit up
straight and unclench.' I gently pulled at her fingers,
smoothing them out. 'Unclench all of you. Now. Relax.
Reeelaaax.'

Treasure giggled. 'You sound like you're hypno-
tizing me now.'

'Well, so what. It's working.'

'Yeah, while you're here. It's when you're *not*.'

'Look, maybe tonight I could come up into the attic
again? I could sleep up here with you. Would you like
that?'

'That would be great.' Treasure suddenly looked
hopeful. 'Or I could maybe creep downstairs and sleep
in your bed with you?'

'No, that's too risky, you know it is. I'll come up into
the attic. It'll be fun, like a sleepover.'

I wasn't sure how I was going to organize things. I
thought I might have to wait till it was really late,
when everyone else had gone to bed, but everything
conspired to make it as easy as anything.

Dad got so drunk he didn't even make it through supper. He ate a few bites of steak, gagged suddenly, and lurched from the room. Mum stared at the salad on her plate, cutting her cucumber and carrot into tiny pieces while Dad threw up noisily in the downstairs loo. Wanda groaned sympathetically, her hand clamped over her mouth. After a long time we heard Dad staggering up the stairs.

Wanda scraped her chair back and got up. Mum glared at her.

'He's ill. Perhaps I'd better help—'

'He'll manage,' said Mum.

So Wanda sat down again. She was greasy-white herself. Her eyes suddenly popped.

'I'm sorry, I . . .' She bolted from the room.

'Dear God,' Mum said, putting her knife and fork down. 'Has she been drinking too?' She sighed heavily.

I felt sorry for her. It was going to be so humiliating when she found out about Wanda's baby. I felt so sad for all of them. It made me feel empty inside. I stuffed a large slice of bread in my mouth to try to ease things.

'Absolutely nothing ever affects your appetite, India,' said Mum.

The bread tasted like cotton wool in my mouth. It swelled up, choking me. I coughed, tears welling.

'Oh for goodness *sake*, India. You're not *crying*, are you?'

I swallowed the wad of bread.

'No, Mum, I'm not crying,' I said firmly. 'Disappointed?'

Mum looked at me. She shook her head but didn't pursue it. 'I've really got to catch up on some work,' said Mum, looking at her watch.

'Well, I'm going to do my homework and have an early night,' I said.

Mum nodded. She patted her cheek for me to kiss. I made noises with my mouth without touching her.

'Night, Mum.'

I cleared the table and stacked the dishwasher, raiding the kitchen for night-time snacks while I was at it. I knew Mum wasn't likely to look in on me when she went to bed, but I arranged some of my old clothes in a heap under the bedclothes, with Edwina Bear across the pillow, just in case. Then I changed into my pyjamas and dressing gown, gathered up all the goodies, crept along the landing and up the ladder.

Treasure had been busy drawing. She'd run out of paper so she'd started to crayon on the walls.

'Um! Treasure, those felt-tips are indelible!'

'But you said no-one ever comes up here.'

'That's true. Still . . .'

'I wanted to feel like Anne Frank. She had stuff all over her walls. Birthday cards and pictures of the Dutch royal family. She thought they were really special, didn't she?'

'So have you drawn William and Harry then?' I said, going to have a look.

'No, you nut! I've drawn all the people who are really special to me. Look. That's you!'

She'd drawn me first, in my school uniform, with a great fuzz of orange hair and scribbly brown clothes. She didn't have a proper flesh shade so she'd coloured me in very pinkly. I wished she hadn't made me look quite so fat, even though I *am*. I looked like a big pink pig who'd been rolling in the mud. Still, I was so pleased she thought me special enough for my portrait to be in pride of place. She'd drawn Nan too, of course, in a tiny white and gold outfit, her arms raised, her legs bent in a complicated manner.

'She's doing a line dance,' said Treasure. 'So's Patsy.'

Patsy was in a little pink top and trousers. It was hard to tell where her clothes ended and her skin began, but she looked very cute.

Treasure had drawn Loretta too, holding a very large baby Britney almost as big as her mother.

'Well, I like Britney more than Loretta,' said Treasure.

She'd drawn Willie on his bike, though it was a pretty weird vehicle, one wheel much bigger than the other.

That was it.

'What about your mum?'

'Don't want her. Or anyone else. *These* are my special people. You do yours now, India, on the opposite wall.'

It felt extraordinary drawing right onto the white

wall. It felt terribly daring at first but I soon got used to it. I drew Treasure first. It sounds like boasting, but I know more about drawing than she does. I can do perspective and shading and vary the line so my people look real. I decided it might be tactful not to make Treasure look *too* real, so I didn't add her scar, I sketched in her glasses very lightly, and I gave her hair an imaginary wash and blow-dry.

'Yeah, I look great,' said Treasure delightedly, hanging over me.

I got out the red felt tip to do her coat but Treasure prized it out of my fingers.

'No, I want to be wearing your mum's clothes, Moya Upton from head to foot.'

'You've no taste, Treasure,' I said, but I obediently drew her in the latest spring designs.

'Cool! You draw them really brilliantly. Maybe you could be a designer like your mum?'

'*No*, thank you very much,' I said. 'Watch it or I'll scribble all over you.'

But I finished Treasure very carefully and neatly, even inventing a new pair of pointy boots with high heels which I knew she'd appreciate.

'Brilliant,' said Treasure. 'I wish you could make them real. Who are you going to draw next?'

I conducted a little audition in my head. Dad failed. And Mum. And Wanda and all the other au pairs. Maria didn't get a look in. Or Ben. And I couldn't even get enthusiastic about Miranda any more.

'I've only got one other special person,' I said.

I drew a mass of dark hair and big dark eyes and a thin face and a pointy chin . . .

'Anne Frank!' said Treasure. 'Hey, why don't you give her some Moya Upton clothes too? She'd look great in them.'

I experimented lightly in pencil but it felt sacrilegious, like drawing a T-shirt and jeans on the crucified Christ. I drew Anne with her little white collar and dark cardigan and checked skirt. I tucked her diary in one hand and her precious fountain pen in the other.

'There! Treasure, are you still keeping your diary?'

'Of course I am. I'm writing heaps and heaps. I've used up nearly all your drawing pad writing it.'

'I'll get you another notebook, don't worry. Hey, I couldn't have just a little peep at some of the stuff you've written, could I?'

'No! It's deadly secret. You show me *yours*.'

'I haven't got it on me, have I? I keep it hidden in my bedroom. Oh go on, Treasure, *please*. Just one page.'

'Not even one *word*, Nosy,' said Treasure, grinning.

'Not even though we're best friends?'

'Absolutely not.'

'How about if I bribe you?' I said, opening up my bag of goodies. 'Kettle chips? Olives? Chocolate raisins?'

'Hey, this is like a real sleepover party, isn't it? We ought to have some scary videos too.'

'We'll tell scary ghost stories to each other instead,' I suggested.

We nibbled companionably, both of us sitting on the camp bed, though we had to be careful to balance the weight. I was acutely conscious of the fact that *my* weight was practically twice Treasure's but she didn't tease me about it at all. I made up a story about a woman being walled up long ago. For days and days afterwards people could hear her scrabbling on the wall with her fingernails. I reached down surreptitiously and trailed my own fingernails over the floorboards, making Treasure jump terribly.

Then she told me several real stories about Terry and what he'd done to her. They were far more scary than my imaginary melodramas.

I'd been dying to go to the loo for ages but I kept putting it off because I felt embarrassed about using the waste bin – but then Treasure used it and so I plucked up the courage to do it too. Then we cuddled down in a nest of clothes and my bedcover and confided all the most embarrassing things that had ever happened to us. I had *heaps* more than Treasure. Then we got on to all our favourite things and the best days of our lives. I told Treasure that the day I met her was one of the best days of my life.

'Yeah, it's one of my best days too,' she said, putting her thin arms round me.

'You're just saying that because *I* said it.'

'No, it's true. I wrote it in my diary. I can't show you, because that book's back at Nan's. But I will show you one *teeny* bit of *this* diary, if you promise not to laugh. I'll show you a picture I drew, OK? Don't laugh, it looks a bit like a valentine.'

I didn't laugh, I nearly cried, when she showed me this beautiful picture of us together enclosed in a heart with roses all around.

She's my best friend ever, ever, ever.

Seventeen

Treasure

I shall have to write in very scrunched up small letters until India gets me that new notebook.

She stayed all night with me. I had a very bad Terry nightmare. He was climbing up into the attic, creeping towards me in the dark, telling me not to be frightened, it would be all over quick as quick and then he pounced. I screamed out loud and India had to put her hand over my mouth to shut me up. She cuddled me until I stopped shivering and then curled up beside me in our nest on the floor.

I didn't go back to sleep for ages – and then when I did I had another dream. It was worse than the Terry one. It was about Nan. It was so *real*. Her arms were tight round me. I could smell her powder and perfume and her long hair tickled my neck as she kissed me goodbye. Then she put me on a train and the door shut with a clang. I couldn't get the window open to give Nan another hug. She mouthed, 'I love you,' and waved, tears rolling down her cheeks. Then the train started moving. Patsy was on the platform, clinging to Nan and waving. I saw Willie and Loretta and Britney and even my mum, but the train was going faster now so they were all a blur. But India ran along the platform, waving and waving, her cheeks scarlet, her hair a great gingery fuzz, but she couldn't keep up. No-one could. The train gathered speed, going faster and faster. Then we suddenly went into a tunnel and it was dark, everything pitch black, and it went on and on and I eventually realized it was going on for ever.

Eighteen

India

Dear Kitty

I set my alarm for five so I could creep back to my room long before anyone was up. Treasure was asleep. I think she was having another bad dream because she kept twitching and groaning. I patted her shoulders gently and she sighed and turned over onto her tummy.

'That's it, Treasure. No more bad dreams,' I whispered, and then I went down the attic steps.

I was feeling thirsty so I slipped downstairs to the kitchen for a glass of milk. Someone was sitting there in the dark! I screamed.

'Hey, hey, sh! It's me, India.'

'Dad? What are you doing? Why are you in the dark?'

189

I switched the light on. Dad blinked at me, his face contorted. His eyes were red, his hair tousled, his pyjamas unbuttoned. He smelt bad too, of drink and sick.

'Switch that light off, for God's sake,' said Dad.

'You should go to bed, Dad. You look awful.'

'I *feel* bloody awful,' said Dad. 'And I can't sleep.'

I felt in the fridge, trying to find the right bottle.

'Would you like a glass of milk, Dad?'

'Absolutely not,' said Dad. He yawned and scratched. 'India, you didn't scream earlier on, did you? I thought I heard something—'

'No, Dad,' I said, sipping milk as nonchalantly as I could.

'Oh well, it was probably a cat yowling.' Dad paused. 'I think I made a bit of a prat of myself at teatime, didn't I?' he said into the dark.

'You weren't very well,' I said kindly.

Dad sighed. 'You can say that again.' His voice was muffled. My heart started beating faster. He might have been *crying*.

'Dad?' I felt my way towards him.

'Oh India, I'm in such a mess,' said Dad. 'It's all going to come out soon. What am I going to do?'

'Have you told Mum?'

'Of course not!'

'Have you talked things over with Wanda?'

'What? No, it's time that silly girl was packed off back to Australia.'

The milk went sour in my mouth. How could he be so callous?

'I think you're hateful to poor Wanda. You've just *used* her.'

'Oh, for God's sake, India, you don't know what you're talking about.'

'Well I don't want to talk about *anything* with you,' I said, and I left him there, sitting in the dark.

I went back to my own bed but I couldn't sleep. When I went back downstairs for breakfast I was relieved that Dad had already left for work. Mum had gone too. It was just Wanda and me. We switched on the portable television and watched the news. Treasure was the third item. She was 'the Latimer Estate girl who is still missing. A thirty-three-year-old man, believed to be a neighbour, is currently helping police with their enquiries.'

'My God, that's so close it's scary,' said Wanda. 'That poor little kid. I wonder if they'll ever find her.'

'Don't talk as if she's dead!'

'It's obvious the police think this guy's murdered her or they wouldn't have arrested him.'

'He's *not* arrested, he's simply helping the police. I'm sure they'll let him go soon.'

I kept seeing poor Mumbly Michael shaking his head and sticking out his tongue. I felt so bad about him. I knew Treasure was right. We had to do something to help him.

School was buzzing with it all when Wanda dropped me off.

'There, India, satisfied?' said Alice, hands on her hips. 'You were getting all shirty with us only the other day, telling us how sweet and lovely everyone is down at the Latimer Estate – and now here's this sweet and lovely rapist and murderer making the news.'

'Rapist? Murderer? What are you on about? There's no proof that any crime at all has been committed. The only *real* crime is that everyone is jumping to stupid conclusions.'

I said it so furiously that Alice took a step backwards.

'There's no need to get so het up, India,' said Maria, putting her arm round Alice.

I glared at them both contemptuously, wondering how I could ever have hung round them, desperate to be their friend. I stalked on, concentrating on my *real* friend.

I'm writing this in an English lesson. We're supposed to be plotting out some stupid story about secrets. I have far more exciting secret plans! I'm *soooo* looking forward to this evening. I'll fix Treasure a real feast. I'll snaffle a big carton of ice-cream out of the freezer and maybe a chocolate cake too. I'll take my tin of beads and coloured threads and we'll make each other special friendship bracelets.

I've got a real present for Treasure too. I'm going to give her the beautiful Italian marble notebook Mum bought me back from Milan. I'd been planning to write my diary in it when this book is finished, but I want to give it to Treasure instead, for *her* diary.

I'll take *this* diary up to the attic too and share it with her. I thought maybe I could write a little passage in *her* diary and she could write in mine. We will share everything . . .

It's all over. Over. Over. Over.

I was writing all those special secret plans in my diary when Mrs Hedges the school secretary came into the classroom and whispered to Mrs Gibbs. Then they both stared at me.

'India, will you go with Mrs Hedges to Mrs Blandford's office, please,' said Mrs Gibbs.

I shut my diary up with a snap and stuck it in my schoolbag quick. I wondered why on earth I had to see Mrs Blandford. She's the headteacher. The only reason you're ever sent to see her is if you're in serious trouble. *Everyone* was staring at me now.

I put my schoolbag over my shoulder and walked out of the classroom after Mrs Hedges.

'What's this all about?' I asked her.

'I'm not sure, dear. This lady came into the school asking if we had any pupils called India. She needs to talk to you.'

I wondered if something awful had happened to Mum or Dad. Maybe I was being punished for writing that I'd like to be an orphan. It suddenly seemed a very sad, scary idea.

I knocked on Mrs Blandford's door and went in.

There was Treasure's nan! She was wearing a smart black suit with a pink jumper but she had no make-up on at all and her hair was pulled back in a straggly ponytail. Her face looked pulled tight too.

Mrs Blandford was leaning forward, her elbows on her desk, her hands making a little arch, fingertips just touching.

'Right, India, come and sit down.'

I did as I was told, looking worriedly at Nan.

'Where's my Treasure?' she said, going straight for it.

'Now then, Mrs . . . ?' said Mrs Blandford.

'I told you, I'm Rita Mitchell, Treasure's nan.'

'And you know India?'

Nan sighed impatiently. 'Yes, I *said*.' She looked at me. 'India?'

'Hello, Nan,' I said weakly.

'And you know this lady's granddaughter, Treasure, too?'

'Yes.'

Mrs Blandford's fingers did a little *tap, tap, tap* against each other.

'Do you know where Treasure is now, India?' said Mrs Blandford.

I didn't know what to do, what to say. It was all so complicated.

'Treasure's all right, Nan, I promise,' I said.

'So where is she then?' said Nan. 'Is she at your home? I know you live at Parkfield – but which road?

194

I've been all over the place, looking for you. Come on, India, tell me your address.'

I swallowed. I knew how badly Treasure wanted to be with Nan but if she went back now she'd still be trapped by Terry. I wanted to keep her safe in the secret attic. I could look after her. Nan hadn't been much use in protecting her from Terry.

'I'm afraid I can't tell you,' I said.

'Oh, for God's sake!' said Nan, standing up and seizing me by the shoulders.

'Please, Mrs Mitchell! Sit down! Leave India *alone*!' said Mrs Blandford.

Nan took no notice. Her bony fingers dug into me.

'Come on, India, tell me! *Is* she at your home? Listen, this has gone on long enough. That poor Michael will be locked up for good before we know where we are and we both know *he's* got nothing to do with it.'

'Mrs Mitchell, I shall have to have you removed if you don't control yourself.' Mrs Blandford skirted her desk and tugged at Nan ineffectually.

'I *can't* control myself! My granddaughter's been missing for days – and she's got asthma, don't you know that, India?' She shook me hard.

'I tried to buy her some Ventolin but they wouldn't sell it to me. It's OK, I can calm her down when she has an attack.'

'For a bright little kid you can be incredibly stupid,' said Nan. She took her hands off my shoulders so abruptly my head jerked backwards. 'What if you *can't*

195

calm her down? An asthma attack isn't like a toddler tantrum. It can be very dangerous.'

'Well, give me her inhaler,' I begged.

'So you *do* know where this missing child is, India?' said Mrs Blandford. She sighed. 'I think we'd better call the police.'

'No! Please don't. I don't know, I don't know,' I said desperately.

'Yes you do – and if something happens to Treasure it will be all your fault!' Nan hissed.

'That's enough!' said Mrs Blandford. 'Sit down, Mrs Mitchell. India, I've phoned your mother. I'll wait until she gets here, but then I think I shall *have* to bring the police in. This is all very serious.'

'You've called my mum?' I said, and I burst into tears.

'Don't cry, India. I didn't mean to be so heavy with you. But I've *got* to find Treasure,' said Nan.

She took hold of me and drew me onto her lap. I flung my arms round her neck and started sobbing down the front of her pink jumper.

'There now. Don't cry so, pet. I'm sorry. I didn't mean it when I said it's your fault. It's *my* fault. I should never have told the kids to stay away for the day. That was just plain stupid. *I'm* stupid. I've handled this all wrong. It's just I haven't slept properly since Saturday. I've been going out of my mind worrying about Treasure.'

Nan held me close and rocked me while I wailed.

Mrs Blandford eyed us very warily, as if her study had been invaded by wild animals.

Then I heard Mum outside, sounding off to Mrs Hedges.

'What on earth is all this about? It's ridiculous. My daughter doesn't know the little girl who's gone missing! She doesn't know anyone on the Latimer Estate.'

Mum barely knocked on the door, sweeping into Mrs Blandford's study, her work glasses pushed on top of her head like an Alice band, a tape measure dangling round her neck.

'For goodness' sake, Mrs Blandford . . .' she started.

Then she saw me, sitting on Nan's lap. 'India! Get up! What are you doing?' Two pink spots flared on Mum's cheeks as if she'd been slapped on either side.

'Come and sit down, Mrs Upton,' said Mrs Blandford, attempting to take control.

Mum stayed standing. She held out her hand to me.

'India, come here!'

I had to slide off Nan's lap. She gave me a little pat as I did so.

'There now, you go to your mum.' Nan nodded at my mum. 'How do you do? I'm Rita Mitchell, Treasure's nan. My Treasure and your India are pals.'

'I'm sorry?' said Mum, pulling me towards her. She put her arm round me awkwardly. I could feel she was shaking. She looked at me. 'You need to wipe your nose, India! Now, tell me, do you *really* know this lady's granddaughter?'

'She's my best friend,' I sniffed, taking Mum's tissue.

'But how do you know her? She doesn't go to this school, does she?'

Mrs Blandford looked appalled. 'No, she doesn't!'

'I'd like to send Treasure here if I could,' said Nan. 'She's a very bright girl.'

'How did you get to know her, India?' said Mum.

'I – I went home from school past their flats.'

'Wanda took you through the Latimer Estate?'

'Wanda wasn't with me.' I felt mean saying it. I didn't want to get Wanda into trouble too.

'You walked through the Latimer Estate all by yourself?' said Mum.

'Yes. And I met Treasure.'

'She's been to tea, dear,' said Nan, bristling at Mum's tone. 'And she came round on Saturday. That was when Treasure first went missing.'

'I didn't know where she was then, I swear,' I said.

'But you do now. You've as good as admitted it,' said Nan. '*Is* she round at your place, India?'

'Of course your granddaughter isn't at my house,' said Mum. 'What sort of family do you think we are? We wouldn't harbour a missing child! This is all some ghastly mistake – isn't it, India?'

I had to shake my head. I didn't want to betray Treasure but I didn't want her to have another asthma attack all by herself. I hadn't realized they could be dangerous. Nan was right. I'd been unbelievably stupid.

'She *is* at home, Mum,' I said.

'*What?*'

'She's been there all the time – but I've looked after her, Nan, I promise I have.'

'What are you *talking* about, India?' said Mum. 'We haven't got any child staying with us.'

'You and Dad and Wanda didn't notice. She's in the secret attic like Anne Frank.'

'She's there *now*?' said Mum.

Nan was already on her feet.

'Let's go and get her!'

So we set off, Mum and Nan and me. Mrs Blandford gave me permission to go. She didn't phone the police. She obviously didn't want the school in the headlines.

'Are *you* going to call the police, Mum?' I asked, as she drove us home.

'I suppose I shall have to,' Mum said, sounding dazed. 'I don't know. I can't get to grips with this. Are you sure this isn't one of your pretend games, India? She *can't* be in the attic.'

'She's been in the attic since *Saturday*?' said Nan.

'It's OK. She's been eating well and I've given her lots of things to do and I've kept her company as much as possible. I spent the whole night with her to stop her being lonely.'

'You slept in our attic?' said Mum. 'You *can't* have. I looked in on you when I went to bed – didn't I? Didn't

Dad? Or Wanda? What is Wanda *playing* at? She's supposed to look after you!'

We gave Wanda a terrible fright when we came barging in through the front door, Mum and Nan and me. She stared at the three of us.

'Oh my lord, what's happened? Is it Richard? Is he sick?' She started shaking.

Mum was so caught up with the whole Treasure thing she didn't seem to find Wanda's concern for Dad at all odd.

'It's India who's sick. Sick in the head. Did you know about this new friend of hers?'

'Oh yes. I thought it was great that she's made a nice friend,' said Wanda. 'Tiffany?'

'Treasure! And you let her play on the *Latimer* Estate?'

'Look, save your argy-bargy for later. Where's *Treasure*?' said Nan.

She started running up the stairs. I ran after her, Mum and Wanda following. Nan got to the attic steps long before us on her strong dancer's legs. She bounded up the ladder and pushed at the trapdoor.

'Treasure? Treasure, are you up there?'

I heard Treasure gasp. 'Nan! Oh Nan!'

When I got up the steps myself Nan was kneeling on the floor with her arms tight round Treasure. Treasure was hugging Nan hard, her face screwed up, sobbing.

'You don't ever cry, Treasure,' I whispered.

She didn't hear me. It was as if Treasure and Nan were in their own little glass dome, sealed off from the rest of us, gold glitter and silver stars whirling all around them.

I had tears in my own eyes.

Mum hauled herself up into the attic too, walking around in a daze, as if she'd arrived on a different planet. She looked at the drawings on the wall, Treasure's bed and tray and bin. She looked at Treasure herself. Then her eyes suddenly focused.

'You're wearing Moya Upton!'

Wanda came halfway through the trapdoor, standing on the steps so that her head poked out into the attic, comically swivelling round and round.

'Come along, Treasure. Time to go home,' said Nan.

'But she can't go home with you!' I said. 'Then she'll have to go back to her mum's and Terry will be there. That's why I hid her. She's got to stay in hiding, don't you *understand*?'

'India! Don't you dare use that tone to Mrs Mitchell,' said Mum.

Nan didn't turn a hair at my tone.

'She can't stay here for ever, pet. You meant it all for the best, I know, but you weren't thinking straight. You got carried away. You can't keep someone hidden indefinitely.'

'Anne Frank stayed hidden.'

'You and that wretched Anne Frank,' said Mum. 'For God's sake, India, grow up.'

'I don't want to grow up,' I cried. 'What's so great about grown ups? Look at you! You all cheat and lie and pretend.'

'That's enough, India,' said Mum. 'There's no need to become hysterical. I can scarcely believe all this. You *can't* have kept Treasure up here for days. We would have noticed.'

'You don't notice anything. You just care about your stupid Moya Upton designs. You don't care one little bit about me. You don't care about Dad either. You haven't got a clue about what's been going on!' I shouted, pacing up and down.

'Will you stop this embarrassing display, India,' said Mum. 'And watch those floorboards. I don't think they'll stand up to you galumphing around like an elephant.'

'That's right! You always have to belittle me, don't you? You do it to everyone – even Dad. No wonder he wants Wanda more than you! She's having his baby – that's something else you haven't noticed.'

Wanda gasped. Mum looked at her. Her lips tightened. But she stayed totally in control.

'You're being ridiculous now, India. Go downstairs. We'll *all* go downstairs and calm down and have a cup of tea. Wanda, can you organize a pot, please, and some juice for the girls.'

Wanda bobbed back down the ladder. Mum followed her, head held high.

'Wow! You really told her!' Treasure whispered, wiping her eyes.

'It's because we're all so het up. Your mum will understand,' said Nan, giving me a pat.

'She won't,' I said, starting to cry. I wished I hadn't

said it. I didn't know what poor Wanda would do now. Or Dad.

'Hey, I'm the cry-baby,' Treasure said. 'Don't cry, India, you'll set me off again.'

'I can't bear it that it's all over. I'll never see you again!'

Treasure left Nan and came and put her arms round me, looking straight into my eyes.

'Of course we'll see each other. We're best friends for ever and ever.'

I hugged her. 'But you'll still have to go back to your Mum and Terry.'

'No, she won't,' said Nan determinedly. 'You wait and see. Trust me, India.'

That was just it. I knew you couldn't trust grown ups, not even kind, truthful ones like Nan.

We went downstairs to the living room and sat down to a bizarre little tea party spread out on the red lacquer table. Mum sat in her cream armchair, asking questions about milk and sugar, rearranging the assorted biscuits on the big black glass plate into a geometric pattern. Wanda hovered in the doorway looking terrified, her hands clasped protectively over her stomach.

Nan and Treasure sat on the sofa together. Nan kept reaching out and touching Treasure as if she was making sure she was real. Treasure sat very upright, her scar showing through her fringe, her eyes blinking hard behind her glasses. She bit into a biscuit and sprayed crumbs down her T-shirt. She caught Mum's eye.

'I'm sorry,' said Treasure, brushing at the crumbs. 'It's your T-shirt.'

'We'll wash all the clothes and send them straight back,' said Nan.

'No, no, please! You keep them, Treasure. They look wonderful on you,' said Mum. She kept staring at Treasure, her head on one side. Then she sighed. 'I suppose I'd better call the police now.'

Nan leant forward. 'I don't think you need to get involved. They'll ask all sorts of awkward questions. They might well think you or your husband had something to do with it. Like you said, you could be done for harbouring.'

'That's ludicrous,' said Mum.

'Is it?' said Nan. 'Most people would find it hard to believe you could have a strange child living in your house for four days and not have a clue she was there.'

Mum flinched.

'It would be better for your India if she could be kept right out of it too,' said Nan.

'No, it wouldn't! I want to talk to the police. I don't mind a bit if *I'm* done for harbouring.'

I saw it all: my impassioned speech straight to camera as I was led away by the police; my interviews with social workers and psychiatrists; my stay in a secure young offenders unit; my secret smuggled letters to Treasure. Then there'd be our joyful reunion, cameras flashing as we embraced outside the unit; my story serialized in the newspapers; my *Secret Attic* book piled high in Waterstone's and Smith's. I'd be a best-selling author before I'd even reached adolescence!

'Be quiet, India. You've said more than enough today,' said Mum. She looked at Nan. 'I would certainly appreciate it enormously if India *could* be kept out of it – but obviously the police will question Treasure.'

'I'll just say I hid by myself,' said Treasure. She looked straight at my Mum. 'I won't say a word about India if you promise something, Mrs Upton.'

Mum looked amused. 'Promise what? That you can have some more Moya Upton clothes?'

Treasure looked at Mum pityingly. 'No! I want you to promise that India and I can still see each other and stay friends.'

'Of course you can,' said Mum. But how can I trust her?

Treasure and Nan said goodbye and went off to the Latimer Estate. Mum offered to drive them but Nan said they needed a little walk to talk things over.

Mum and Wanda and I were left alone together.

'I don't know what I'm going to do with you, India,' Mum said weakly. 'I don't think I can talk about it now. I need time to think. Wanda, will you drive India back to school, please?'

Wanda leapt to her feet, eager to postpone an inevitable confrontation.

'Come along, India,' she said. Then she glanced out of the living-room window and stood transfixed. She

205

pointed mutely with one long fingernail. A police car had drawn up outside.

'Oh no,' said Mum. 'How did they find out?'

But they weren't here because of Treasure. Dad got out of the back of the police car. One of the police officers was holding his arm. Wanda gasped. Mum sighed heavily.

'Dear God, what is it now?'

Dad led the police officers into the house. He was very red in the face, not looking at anyone, staring down at the black carpet.

'What's happened, Dad?' I whispered.

Mum stood up, folding her arms. She looked at the police.

'Have you *arrested* my husband?'

'No, madam, not at this present moment in time. Mr Upton is simply helping us with our enquiries. Now, sir, if we could go to your study perhaps you can show us where all the relevant papers are?'

The accountants had discovered a large amount of money had gone missing from Major Products. It looked as if Dad was going to be charged with embezzlement.

Nineteen

Treasure

Nan and I walked back to Latimer together, hand in hand. No-one paid us any attention as we walked down Parkfield's leafy avenues. I'd had my photo all over the newspapers and on the telly but it simply didn't register. Cars whizzed past us on the main road. A police car even stopped for us at the zebra crossing. Nan and I nodded and smiled. No-one gave us a second look.

Maybe it was the Moya Upton clothes. They made me look so different.

'Are Mum and Terry still at your place, Nan?' I asked.

'They're gone. This paper's done a deal – a fifty-thousand-pound exclusive – so they're hidden away in some hotel, with Kyle and Bethany and Gary. God, that baby grizzles so. He might be my grandchild but I can't take to him at all.'

'He's my brother but I don't like him either,' I said.

I held on tight to Nan's hand as if I was a little kid.

'He takes after his dad,' she said. She gave my hand a squeeze. 'You're not going back to them, Treasure. I don't give a damn what anyone says. I don't care about all these silly social workers who keep telling me grandparents rarely get custody. Blow them – and blow your mum's solicitors too. If they see my Pete as the problem then he'll simply have to live somewhere else when he comes out the nick.'

I stood stock still, staring up at Nan. Her blue eyes blazed at me. Her ponytail band had fallen out and her blond hair was blowing in the wind, lifting up around her head like a wild halo.

'But you love Pete, Nan,' I whispered.

'I know I do. But I love you too, Treasure. As much as any of my own kids – maybe even more, though don't you dare tell anyone that. It's been agony, wondering if you were all right. I should have told them at the hospital how you got that cut. I should have gone straight down the Social then. I shouldn't have packed you off on Saturday, though I just wanted to keep you out of any rows with Terry. I've been such a fool but I'm going to fight for you now, darling. I let that pig dribble on about his little Treasure, hamming it up for the cameras. I knew the time to have *my* say was when you came back safe and sound. I'll tell all those journalists and telly people what he's really like.'

I tugged on Nan's hand.

'*I'll* tell them, Nan.'

Everything went crazy the moment we set foot on the Latimer Estate. People knew me there. They started shouting when they spotted us. Little kids came running. Even old ladies hobbled up and circled us, acting awestruck, like I'd come back from the dead. We had a huge troop following us when we got to Elm block.

There was a television van parked beside the skateboard ramp, and several reporters and photographers were drinking tea together. The police were still there too, in overalls and rubber gloves, sifting through every stinking sack of rubbish in the dustbin recess.

Nan and I stood there, still hand in hand. We watched them all. One of the reporters was eyeing up Nan – and then he looked at me. His head jerked. He glanced at the busy police and then came sprinting towards us.

'It's Treasure! You're safe and sound! Where have you been, darling? Come on, be a sweetheart and tell me quick.'

Another reporter came running, elbowing him out the way.

'No, no, we've got an exclusive! Come with me, lovie. We've got your mum and dad and the kids tucked away in a safe hotel. You're to come with us.'

A photographer started taking photos, telling me to look up, look down, to smile, while his flash made orange blurs in my eyes.

The police looked up from the dustbins and they came running too.

'Is that the little girl? Leave her alone, chaps, come on. This way, Treasure,' said a policeman.

They were all milling round, shouting, gesturing, flashing – and then a man with a television camera was there too, and a guy with headphones and a boom and another with a mike, asking me endless questions. They were all arguing, telling me to go this way, that way. It was all so loud, so noisy, so unreal, as if I was in some crazy cartoon. I clung to Nan, the only real person there.

She put her head down to me. 'Where do *you* want to go, Treasure?'

'Back home with you!' I said, loud and clear.

'OK, pet,' she said. 'Tell them.'

The journalists were still all yelling at me, the police were trying to usher me out their way, the television people had their mike thrust right in my face. I'd never have a better chance to have *my* say.

'I want to live with my nan,' I said. 'I saw on the telly that Michael next door has been questioned. That's mad. He didn't take me away. No-one did. I ran away myself. I've been hiding for days and it's because I don't want to live with my mum. I don't get on with my stepdad. They say I've got to come back but I don't want to. I've been living with my nan since Christmas and I want to *stay* here. *Please* – please, please, please can I stay with my nan?'

It was all over every paper the next day – except the

one that did the exclusive deal with Terry. LITTLE TREASURE TELLS HER STORY! I had to do lots and lots of telling. To the police. To the social workers. To more journalists.

One newspaper started a special campaign: *A Child's Right to Choose*. A magazine for senior citizens interviewed Nan about 'Granny's rights'. There was a phone-in on local radio and a piece on *Woman's Hour*. Then Nan and I went on the *Esther* show and we were interviewed on *This Morning*. I didn't say *too* much about Terry on television. I just made it plain I couldn't stick him. I loved my mum but I loved my nan *more*. I simply wanted to live with her. I said it over and over and over again.

AND IT WORKED!

Nan and I had to go to a very scary meeting with lots of senior social workers. Mum was there too. Not Terry. He'd been invited but he said he wasn't going to sit down like some silly schoolkid and be bossed about by stupid social workers. Or words to that effect. He was furious because he'd lost his £50,000 exclusive deal – *and* one of the other newspapers had done some research and interviewed one of his ex-girlfriends who said he'd often beaten her up and terrified her kids.

I was so relieved I didn't have to see him. It was very upsetting seeing Mum though. I felt really, really bad. She was so angry with me.

'How could you do this to us, Treasure? Telling everyone you don't give a toss about your own mum!

211

Dragging our names through the mud so we can't go anywhere now without folk staring and whispering. One guy even spat at my Terry, calling him scum. I don't care what you say, he's been a good dad to you in lots of ways, and I've tried my hardest to be a good mum too, even though you've never been an easy kid to get on with. You've always looked down your nose at us, haven't you, you snotty little cow. Well, you live with your nan if that's what you want. We'll be better off without you, me and Terry and the kids. We don't love you any more. We don't want you any more, see.'

When the meeting was over Mum walked off like she wasn't even going to say goodbye to me. I ran after her quick.

'Mum, please. *I* still love *you*,' I said.

'Well, you've got a funny way of showing it, acting like I'm total rubbish,' Mum said fiercely – but she suddenly hugged me hard.

'You be a good girl, Treasure. You're still *my* girl, no matter what,' she whispered in my ear.

I couldn't help wanting to hang on to her. It was almost as if I wanted to go back with her, even after all I'd gone through. I knew she couldn't look after me. I felt I should really be looking after her.

'I feel so bad, Nan. She *is* my mum.'

'I know, pet. She's my daughter. But I can't think about what's best for her now. I have to think about what's best for *you*.'

So I went back to live with Nan. It was all a bit crazy that first week, reporters still rushing round everywhere. And Mrs Watkins came along the balcony and gave me a terrible mouthful as if I'd been the one to accuse her Michael. He didn't seem to bear me any grudge though. He waves and smiles at me behind his mum's back, though she won't let him talk to me now.

The social workers haven't given this new arrangement their full approval. They're going to review the situation every six months. I know it will be sticky when Pete gets out of prison. I'm not sure Nan really would choose me rather than him. He's Patsy's *dad*. But I'm safe with Nan for a while. Maybe you can't always make people promise for ever and ever.

India says she'll always hide me away again somewhere. Not in the secret attic. Their house is up for sale. But Moya says they won't move far away. She needs to stay near her studio. And India and I *can't* lose touch, not now I work for her mother.

I am the new Moya Upton model!

India doesn't mind, even though she hates Moya's clothes herself. She says they look OK on me. *I* think they look f-a-n-t-a-s-t-i-c. We've done photo shoots for *Vogue* and *Tatler*. Moya doesn't mind me being pale and skinny. She doesn't even mind my funny eyes and the scar. I got worried when the *Guardian* newspaper did an article about the dangers of stick-thin street-kid waifs being used as child models. I thought Moya might drop me and go back to using that Phoebe as her main model but she said it was all good publicity.

213

India sighed and rolled her eyes – but she wasn't getting at *me*.

We are still best ever friends. And we always will be. Won't we, India?

Yes yes yes yes yes yes yes yes yes yes yes yes yes yes yes yes yes yes yes!

Twenty

India

Dear Kitty

No, this is silly. I don't need a fictional friend any more. Treasure is my friend. She always will be. Isn't that right, Treasure?

Yes yes yes yes yes yes yes yes yes yes yes yes yes yes yes yes yes yes yes!

I am writing my diary round at Treasure's home. It's lovely to be able to call it that. Later on we're both going to Nan's Friday night line-dancing class. Patsy comes too. She is *brilliant* at it, much, much better than us. Treasure is quite good at it, though she gets her lefts and rights mixed up sometimes. I thought I would be hopeless. I've never been able to get the hang of disco dancing. I've lumbered around at school discos, waggling my arms about (and my bottom too, unfortunately) looking incredibly stupid. I just didn't have a clue how to do it. But line dancing is entirely different. You don't make it up as you go along. You learn every single step, every wave of the arm and stomp and clap and kick. You learn until the sequence becomes a little pattern in your head and your feet automatically obey.

I am light on my feet too, even though I'm so heavy. It doesn't matter a bit if you're fat. There's a couple of ladies at Nan's class who are *huge* but they're still great dancers. There are *old* ladies too, but you should see them wiggle and strut, while the men whistle. Some of the men are quite old too but Jeff and Steve are young and they wear matching checked cowboy shirts and real cowboy boots with steel tips and they dance up a storm. That is the particularly good thing about line dancing. It doesn't matter what sort of person you are, old or young, boy or girl. You just go along and have fun. It is a fantastic feeling when we're all stomping along together through each song.

I have never felt in step with anyone else before. Nan says I'm doing very nicely indeed for a beginner. She sometimes puts me at the front so the others can copy me. But you have to concentrate hard all the time. If you think about anything else you forget the sequence and stumble. That's another especially good thing about line dancing. You can't dwell on your worries.

I've got quite a few worries at the moment. That's

216

why I haven't been writing in my diary recently. I haven't really wanted to write about everything. I've *talked* about it. I've told Chris.

That is another extraordinary thing. I am *in love*.

This is totally private. I am writing with my hand over the page because I don't even want Treasure to know. I am supposed to tell Chris everything but I can't tell him *that*.

I tell him everything else though, and how I feel about it. My mum and dad are splitting up. Sometimes I feel as if I'm splitting in two as well. Other times I don't care at all. I can't help it that they've made a mess of their lives. I just don't want them to make a mess of my life too.

I still love Dad best even now, but I'm going to live with Mum most of the time. I couldn't live with Dad because he's renting a studio flat now and it's much too small. And maybe he doesn't want me around too much because it would cramp his style with his girl-friends. I think he's started seeing *Suzi*. He is totally disgusting. Sometimes I think he almost deserves to go to prison.

The police let him go after they charged him. Dad's got a super-sharp lawyer who's sure he'll get him off the embezzlement charge, no bother at all. Mum thinks she'll have to pay his legal bills. I suppose this is very generous of her.

I asked Mum if she thought Dad had really stolen the money from Major Products.

'Of course not, India! It's all a ludicrous mistake.

Dad got a bit muddled with his accounts, that's all.'

But I heard them having heaps of rows about it, night after night before Dad moved out. Mum didn't say anything about muddles and mistakes. She kept asking him what he'd done with all the money, and had he really just frittered it away on girls and good times?

I know one thing. Dad didn't give poor Wanda a good time.

Wanda disappeared. Mum said she wasn't very well and had to go to a special clinic for a rest. I think I know exactly what happened at this special clinic. I think they got rid of Wanda's baby. I said as much to Mum. She said I've been watching too many soaps on television and insisted Wanda wasn't ever pregnant. I don't believe Mum. I can't ask Wanda. As soon as she was well enough to leave the clinic she went back to Australia. Mum paid her air fare.

Mum's having to sell the house because she's had to pay for so much. She says it's time to move on anyway. We're probably going to live in a flat, just the two of us. Not a Latimer Estate sort of flat. Mum wants us to live in a Victorian mansion block near her work. It's still *quite* near here, though it's too far to go to my school. I'm not sure Mrs Blandford would want me to stay on anyway. It was her idea to send me to the educational psychologist. She obviously thinks I'm some kind of nutcase. Mum does too.

But *Chris* says I'm the sanest person he's ever met. And I'm boasting again now, but he *also* says I'm one of the brightest. He's given me an IQ test. It would be gross to tell you the exact number, but if the average IQ is 100 then I have enough intelligence for one and a half people. Mum asked him if I stood a chance of getting a scholarship to one of the posh, big girls' schools and he said I shouldn't have any problems at all.

Chris is the educational psychologist. I see him once a week and it is *wonderful*. I was dreading seeing him the first time. I thought he'd be some suspicious old man with a funny accent and a probing manner. But Chris is twenty-five and he actually looks a lot younger in his jeans and T-shirt. He's not really what you might call good-looking. He's got this really great smile though and freckles all over his face and fuzzy ginger hair. It's *exactly* like my hair.

'Hi, Ginger Twin,' he said, grinning. 'Now, I've always *hated* my hair but it looks great on you.'

'Do people always think you've got a terrible temper?' I asked.

'You bet. It's so tiresome. Maybe I'll get round to doing a special research project on red hair and temperament.'

If Chris doesn't do it, I will. I have decided that I'm going to be a psychologist too. We have long, long, long talks on psychology every week. It's a fascinating way of studying human behaviour. You do it all very scientifically, with experiments. There have been lots and lots of studies ôn family behaviour and what makes a good or bad parent.

Although it's difficult to make up your mind. Perhaps psychology can't ever be an *exact* science. Even the worst parent in the world can be good some of the time.

Anne Frank wrote that she didn't love her mother at all but when they were in the concentration camp they clung together, inseparable.

Mum took Treasure and me to see Anne Frank's house! OK, she was spending a weekend in Amsterdam anyway doing a photo-shoot. Treasure got kitted out in Moya Upton from head to foot. She got made up whiter than ever, with smudged circles under her eyes. She struck scary poses in cobbled streets by the canals while I sat reading an A-level psychology book and eating Dutch apple cake. When Mum and the photographer and the stylist had finished with Treasure at long last, Mum took us to 263 Prinsengracht where Anne hid in the secret annexe. We heard the Westertoren clock strike as we went into the museum, just as Anne describes in her diary.

My heart started beating hard as we went up the narrow stairs and saw the bookcase door. It was all just as I'd imagined it. I stepped into Anne's bedroom and there were her cards and photos still stuck up on the wall. I cried then. So did Treasure.

We saw Anne's red-and-white checked diary too. We couldn't read her neat Dutch handwriting but we didn't need to. We know her story off by heart.

ABOUT THE AUTHOR

JACQUELINE WILSON is one of Britain's most
outstanding writers for young readers. She is the
most borrowed author from British libraries and
has sold over 20 million books in this country.
As a child, she always wanted to be a writer and
wrote her first 'novel' when she was nine, filling
countless exercise books as she grew up. She started
work at a publishing company and then went on
to work as a journalist on *Jackie* magazine (which
was named after her) before turning to writing
fiction full-time.

Jacqueline has been honoured with many
of the UK's top awards for children's books,
including the Guardian Children's Fiction
Award, the Smarties Prize, the Red House Book
Award and the Children's Book of the Year.
She was awarded an OBE in 2002 and is the
Children's Laureate for 2005-2007.

ABOUT THE ILLUSTRATOR

NICK SHARRATT knew from an early age that he wanted to use his drawing skills as his career, so he went to Manchester Polytechnic to do an Art Foundation course. He followed this up with a BA (Hons) in Graphic Design at St Martin's School of Art in London from 1981-1984.

Since graduating, Nick has been working full-time as an illustrator for children's books, publishers and a wide range of magazines. His brilliant illustrations have brought to life many books, most notably the titles by Jacqueline Wilson.

Nick also writes books as well as illustrating them.

JACKY DAYDREAM

Jacqueline Wilson -
The Story of Her Childhood

Illustrated by Nick Sharratt

Everybody knows Tracy Beaker, Jacqueline Wilson's
best-loved character. But what do they know about the
little girl who grew up to become Jacqueline Wilson?

How she played with paper doll like April
in *Dustbin Baby*.

How she dealt with an unpredictable father
like Prue in *Love Lessons*.

How she chose new toys in Hamleys like Dolphin
in *The Illustrated Mum*.

How she sat entrance exams like Ruby in *Double Act*.

But most of all how she loved reading and writing stories.
Losing herself in a new world was the best possible way
she could think of spending her time. From the very
first story she wrote, *Meet the Maggots*, it was clear that
this little girl had a very vivid imagination.

Now her fans can discover a little more about Jacky
herself in this utterly captivating, charming and
poignant memoir.

'Literary superstar' INDEPENDENT

DOUBLEDAY
978 0 385 61015 5

THE ILLUSTRATED MUM
Jacqueline Wilson

Illustrated by Nick Sharratt

Star used to love Marigold, love me, love our life together.
We three were the colourful ones, like the glowing pictures
inked all over Marigold...

Covered from head to foot with glorious tattoos,
Marigold is the brightest, most beautiful mother in the
world. That's what Dolphin thinks (she just wishes her
beautiful mum wouldn't stay out partying all night or
go *weird* now and then.) Her older sister, Star, isn't so
sure any more. She loves Marigold too, but sometimes
she just can't help wishing she were more normal...

A powerful and memorable tale for older readers.

From Jacqueline Wilson, the award-winning author
of *The Suitcase Kid, Double Act, Bad Girls*
and many other titles.

'Powerfully portrayed, sometimes shocking but
ultimately uplifting' BOOKSELLER

'A marvellous, poignant tale...Jacqueline Wilson's
best yet' DAILY TELEGRAPH

SHORTLISTED FOR THE WHITBREAD AWARD

A CORGI YEARLING BOOK
978 0440 86368 7